I0642656

Mysterious Girl Publishing Presents:

BY ANY MEANS...

BY: C. TANAE

BY ANY MEANS

Revised by: C. Tanae

Edited by: C. Tanae

Text formation by: C. Tanae

Cover Concept by: C. Tanae

Back Cover Concept: C. Tanae

ISBN: 0692333215
ISBN 13: 9780692333211
Library of Congress Control Number: **XXXXX (If applicable)**
LCCN Imprint Name: **City and State (If applicable)**

This story is a work of fiction. Any resemblance to real people, living or dead, actual events, establishment and/or locales. Intended to give the reader a sense of reality. Names, Characters, Places, and events are totally coincidental. All words in the story are products of the Authors Imagination and are used fictitiously, as are those fictionalized events. Incidents that involve real persons and did not occur or are set to occur in the future.

Acknowledgements:

First and foremost I give all thanks to The Lord above.
(MOM) I know it's been hard dealing with someone like
myself. Thank you for everything you have ever done and the
things you didn't do. (To my Favorite Aunt) thanks for your
advice and your time listening to me whine about my life.
Thank you call me sometimes I miss you. (Brother) I could
never repay you for your kind ways. You have always been
there for my kids and I. Thank you so much I wish you and
your family the best. I would like to thank my best friend
C. Loyalty is hard to come by and I found that in you. I
would also like to give a special thanks. To the many
Authors that I have reached out to for advice. Thank you
from the bottom of my heart. {You know who you are}. I
would like to thank myself for staying real and honest with
my life and the things that has happen to me that lead me
to write By Any Means & By Any Means Necessary… The late
night writing sections the times I wanted to give up, burn
my story and break the computer. My thought process and my
motivation that brought me through. I would like to thank
everyone that brought pain and suffering that lead me to
write By Any Means.. Coming soon By Any Means Necessary… To
all that didn't believe in me wanted to see me fail.

Mysterious Girl Publishing

Presents:

By Any Means...

Coming soon another Mysterious Girl Publishing:

By Any Means Necessary...

C. Tanae

To my 3 precious Angels that has always seen perfection in me.

May GOD bless you with all your hopes, dreams and desires of your heart.

Always and forever, today, tomorrow and yesterday.

Love always, C. Tanae { You 3 are my life }

Chapter 1: Candy and Sapphire...

Candy was riding in her purple car with her friend Sapphire. Candy seen Rayshawn standing outside the projects on 301st. Candy has always knew of Rayshawn better known as Ray. However Candy hadn't seen him in a long time. Tall black and always had a mean look on his face. Candy told Sapphire. Ray was on his mother house phone. Candy knew the number so she called.

Ring, Ring, Ring

Ray answered after the third ring.

Ray: Hello

Candy: Hi Rayshawn its Candy.

Ray: What's up?

Candy: What's good I haven't seen you in a long time? Where have you been hiding? Candy asked Ray.

Ray: Oh just around.

Candy: Give me your number and I will call you sometimes. They exchanged numbers and hung up.

Candy told Sapphire I can't wait until he calls me girl. Sapphire had her own plan in motion. Sapphire really did care for Candy. However Sapphire would step on anyone toes for some dick. Thinking that a nigga would wife her. Would she cross her only friend Candy?

About 2 days later Rayshawn called Candy and they talked about everything laughed and decided that Ray would come and get her. The next day Ray went to Candy's apartment to get her. Ray drove a Nissan Sentra with lots of music and rims 2 doors. When Ray pulled up Candy came out smiling and got into the front seat.

Ray was taking Candy back to his apartment. Ray was cooking steak with all the sides. Candy and Ray talked at that time Ray was explaining that he had just got out of a 5 year relationship with some girl he never did say her name. The girl had left him with the apartment they once shared. Ray sounded and looked very hurt Candy just listen to him talk. Sometimes it's best to listen to someone talk. Candy was observing Ray apartment nice leather section, nice entertainment center that filled the whole wall Ray apartment is very nice and clean Candy thought. 4 hours later Ray took Candy back to her apartment.

Ray and Candy talked on the phone for the next week. Ray was a really nice guy. Ray eventually went back and picked Candy up they rode around the City listening to music. Ray took Candy back to his apartment where they laid around and enjoyed each other company Ray and Candy went on like this for the next 4-5 months. Candy started leaving items over Ray house without his knowledge. During this time Candy started a job at a clothing store name

Kayla's that sold all name brand clothing. Candy was determined to get money become Rayshawn wife and move into his apartment all without his consent.

Chapter 2: Candy and Sapphire...

Candy and Sapphire had been friends for a very long time. Candy always cared about Sapphire. Sapphire was really book smart and had no knowledge of the street life or the games that dudes would play and the lies they would tell to get some pussy. Candy always looked after Sapphire and loved her like a sister. Candy only had 1 brother named Davion. Davion was a star Quarterback in High School. Davion always wanted to make his family happy. Davion was an Honor Roll student and always did the right things. Candy was just a black sheep growing up. That is how she met Sapphire they lived in the same hood. Sapphire lost contact with Candy when her family moved away. However they were reunited once Sapphire moved back. Sapphire and Candy would do everything together get their nails done, club, drink, ride around whatever. Sapphire was envious of Candy. Candy always knew that Sapphire was sneaky and would fuck anyone boyfriend, husband behind their back. Candy was telling Sapphire girl Ray finally called me and we have been hanging out and everything. Candy was telling Sapphire about Ray's apartment and her plans of moving in and becoming Ray's wife. Sapphire was saying she wish she would have met Rayshawn first. Candy could hear the jealousy in Sapphire voice. Candy felt that Sapphire was loyal to their friendship. Would Candy find out Sapphire wasn't? Candy said damn hoe don't tell me I have to watch you around Ray. I mean really you're my girl and I will never ever think of you as nothing else. Bitch don't try me matter of fact I don't know if Ray and I will ever get serious Candy stated. Sapphire just was very quiet and was thinking BITCH I want Ray to myself and I will get him By Any Means... Candy knew Sapphire was thinking something she just never knew what was running through Sapphire mind.

Chapter 3: Candy and Ray...

It was Ray's birthday Candy and one of Ray friends were over to his apartment. Ray ex-girlfriend came by to wish him a Happy Birthday. Candy was hot and heated you know mad to the EXTREME. Candy knew now was not the time to show how she was truly feeling. They haven't even had sexual intercourse yet.

Ray was very respectful to his friendship with Candy. Ray stepped outside and said something to his ex-girlfriend and she left. Candy was sure she was PISSED when Ray came back in. Candy wasn't mad anymore. Candy heart was beating fast like an excited kid that had just receive her first back at CHRISTMAS. Candy knew for a fact she not only wanted Rayshawn but needed him to be hers and only hers. Ray birthday night they had sex it was so good to Candy. After a couple of drinks, some weed and more sex. Of course Candy gave Ray some smoking ass head you know the type of head that makes your PUSSY wet. When you know it's good to the RECEIVER. Candy and Ray went on having sex and chilling like this for the next 6-7 months. Candy was still working at Kayla's hanging out at the club and going to Ray apartment as soon as the club let out. Candy wasn't having sex with anyone else. Candy was falling head first for Rayshawn in a major way. There was no way that Candy could let Ray know how she was really feeling about him. Candy loved him already Candy knew from the time she seen Ray on the phone that she would love him. Candy knew for a fact if she told Ray that would only scare him away.

Candy was giving Ray nice hallmark cards, money, sex and head. This is where Candy went wrong. Candy confuse not only Ray but herself as well. Candy went to believing something that it wasn't between them Candy was fooling herself. Ray wasn't her boyfriend Ray wasn't nothing at all to Candy. Candy was blinded by her feelings. She couldn't see that the nigga had no intentions on making her his wife or did he?

Chapter 4: Candy and Ray...

7 months later Candy started busting out windows and tires acting CRAZY as heck. Something close to a TAZMANIA DEVIL. Candy had no understanding about nothing when it came to Ray. No one in Ray family had a clue about why Candy was acting the way she was acting with him. Ray was telling everyone that Candy was CRAZY. Ray was acting as if he had no dealings with Candy behind closed doors. Candy was chasing Ray down when he was with other girls. Busting windows every other day soon as Ray would get them fix she would bust them again. One would have thought Ray had a contract with the glass company. Ray ended up going to jail for 6 months. Candy stood by Ray the whole 6 months. Letters, cards, money, visits, phone calls even fussing with his family members. Ray was really close with some of his family members. They would see no wrong in Ray no matter what he did or who he did it to. Candy never slacked when it came to Ray and doing time with him. Candy loved Ray so much. The night before Ray had to turn his self into the County jail they had the most amazing sex. The best ever Ray still didn't give Candy any oral sex. She wanted some head how could she tell Ray? All the times Candy had sucked Ray dick. She had sucked his dick so much she could taste Ray cum from his dick when he wasn't around. That was a lot of sucking. Ray was gone 6 months Candy kept her job, hung out with Sapphire and moved to another apartment in the same Apartment Complex Ray lived in with his ex-girlfriend. The same furniture they once shared Ray would eventually share with Candy.

Candy and Ray was getting serious. Candy believed the 6 months she was doing with Ray showed Ray that she was loyal & cared about him. Ray once told Candy I know it's hard. He will be home soon and he would show Candy how to make 15 cents into a dollar. Ray told Candy to just hold your head up and hold things together for me. Ray told her I want to be with you I care for you Candy I love you he told her. Candy held onto every word like it was her last words she would hear before she died. Even if she didn't have a clue as to what Ray was talking about when he said he is going to show her how to make 15 cents into a dollar. What was he talking about Candy thought?

Little did Ray know when he was Incarcerated Candy was talking to this dude Mark. Candy had told Mark about Rayshawn that he was incarcerated for 6 months. One night Ray had called Candy's phone and Mark answered the phone. Candy had no clue that Mark had answered the phone when Ray had called. When Candy found out what Mark had did. She thought to herself why would Mark answer my phone? Candy told Mark he can stay over her house. Without Mark knowing his body would never be the same. Why Mark was sleeping Candy boiled some hot water and throw on Mark's back. To be HONEST Candy wanted to kill Mark. Ray had stopped calling for a week. All she could do was cry and stress. One thing she knew is that people in jail find things out before the News Paper Company does. Candy knew for a fact that Ray knew everything. What is Ray going to do Candy thought?

Chapter 5: Candy and Ray...

Ray finally got out of the County Jail around 9 am. Ray dad Mr. Jones went and picked him up. Candy had been crying all night long. She didn't know if Ray was coming home to her. Ray said he was coming to the Apartment that Candy had got for them. Candy was the happiest person in the world when she heard a knock on the door. Happier than winning a half of million dollars so you know that's happy. First Ray had to go and spend time with his family. Especially Mrs. and Mr. Jones. Ray was all hers Candy thought finally everything she had done had finally paid off. Candy thought everything Ray had wrote he meant. Every single word Candy loyalty and love had paid off. In the back of Candy's mind she was AFRAID. AFRAID of what? Candy thought to herself AFRAID of killing Ray if he ever tried to be with another chick.

Candy and Ray finally had sex and he gave her some head. Ray head was good well good enough to satisfy her pussy. Than out of the blue Ray clicked and started chocking hitting and kicking on Candy. Candy started to cry asking Ray why? Ray was looking in Candy's eyes all Ray said was BITCH you drugged me for 6 fucking months why I was in jail. Candy was afraid to ask how? Candy was thinking she did everything visit, letters, cards, money, pictures everything. What was he talking about? Candy thought as tears rolled down her face. Candy sexed Ray good showed loyalty and love what more could she have done? Candy thought I should just leave Ray and this Apartment. Candy loved Ray and she wasn't going to leave not even after the signs were there that she should just walk away. If a dude knock the shit out of you one time trust and believe you're going to get it again and again. Could Candy change Ray? Would Candy become another victim? Things between Ray and Candy was moving FAST.

Chapter 6: Candy...

Candy had no clue how much Ray was worth or how much dope Ray was moving. Candy was sleeping with a kingpin without even knowing Candy was blind to the FACT. Candy would later fine out that Ray was moving kilos and kilos of cocaine. One day Ray came home with 80,000 dollars in a garbage bag and 2 kilos of cocaine. Candy had no clue if the police ran up in their Apartment they would both be under a Federal Building they would never see the light of day again. As Candy thought back she realize this is what he meant by turning 15 cents to a dollar. Candy knew when she seen the kilos and the money. Ray had to trust her with everything. Candy told Ray I think we should get a house. Ray agreed and move Candy into a big nice 6 bedroom 3 bathrooms 2 story brick mansion. Candy was able to décor the whole house the way she wanted to with Ray money. Candy brought name brand everything such as Gucci silver wear, China, Northland, and Vividus. Rayshawn had already fell hard for Candy. Ray had a different way of showing her that he loved her. Ray allowed her to buy whatever she wanted to buy. Candy would later find out that she would always have to pay the price? Would it all be worth it at the end? Ray had to take a trip to Mexico to meet with the Mexican Cartel. Candy would never go or ask too many questions. The less she knew the better off she was Candy thought to herself.

Candy and Sapphire hadn't hung out in a long time. Candy called Sapphire up and invited her over to her and Ray's new home. Once Sapphire arrived Candy could see that Sapphire was amazed with everything inside the home and outside. Candy told Sapphire girl I will never forget you no matter what. Were in this together I'm on and you're on as well. Ray money is my money and my money is your money Candy loved Sapphire just that much. If you need anything Sapphire come to me and ask me. No matter what it is Sapphire I'm serious. With that said Sapphire told her thanks I love you thank you so much. Would Candy own words bite her in the ass? Candy knew that Ray never liked Sapphire. Candy and Sapphire went to the best restaurants, shopped at the most expensive stores, and Candy rode in nothing but the best cars, and trucks with Sapphire on her side. Compliments of Ray Candy didn't know the stories that she had shared about Ray was getting Sapphire panties wet. Candy and Sapphire talked about everything. Candy stories were juicier because Ray had money, good sex and moved kilos and kilos of cocaine. Candy already knew the lifestyle Ray had her living many chicks would flock to Ray. Would Ray leave Candy for a chicken head? If it was one person Candy knew that she could trust around Ray and talk to about anything it was Sapphire. Would Sapphire betray Candy? Out of the blue Sapphire started to act funny with Candy. Candy already knew what Sapphire had done. Candy was sitting in her king size bad crying thinking to herself. Why? Why? Why would Sapphire cross her like this? How could she Candy thought? After everything Candy had done for her. Candy would have thought that Sapphire would know and see with her own two eyes that Ray wasn't going to leave Candy. Ray had fed Sapphire a 5 course meal and she ate it up like her life was depending on it. Sapphire not realizing that she was getting fucked and played all the way around the board. Ray fed her lies like he would leave Candy. You know all the bullshit niggas tell a jump off a BITCH that is willing to fuck and suck for pennies on the dollar. One day Sapphire would get the shock of her life. In the meantime Candy wipe her tears away and called Sapphire.

Ring, Ring, Ring

Candy: Hi Sapphire what's up girl?

Sapphire: Nothing what's going on?

Candy: I called you to tell you that you should have stuck with those books in School and went to College. You can't walk in my shoes if you wanted to. You just had to fuck Ray damn shame hoes going to be hoes and niggas are going to fuck. You just became another number to Ray many of hoes. If Ray is over there let him know I love him and he can come home always. With that said Candy hung up the phone.

No one ever knew that Candy was holding a card (INFORMATION) that would change everyone life. Stinky ass bitch should have left well enough alone Candy thought. Sapphire you just had to fuck Ray didn't you? Candy said out loud poor Sapphire poor little Sapphire you should have just stayed my friend. I knew you was jealous of me and I should have just ended our friendship. With those thoughts Candy laughed a little rolled over and took her daily meds.

No one would ever find out Candy secret or would they???

Chapter 7: Candy:

Reminiscing;

Damn bitch Candy was thinking about Sapphire the next morning and what her and Ray had done. Candy thought how could she betray me? Candy would think of Sapphire as dead from that day forward. Candy never told anyone about her family. Not even Ray growing up things were really hard. Candy mother Lauren had 4 children. 2 sons and 2 Daughters. Candy had a much older brother she never met, & a younger sister that she had never laid eyes on. Lauren would beat Candy with extension cords for jumping out the window going with different dudes and stealing her car. Candy mother was so tired of her she sent Candy to live with her Grandma her Grandma was really mean. Candy Grandma use to beat her with a switch you know the part of a tree branch. When Candy was 13 she had a baby girl that situation would only complicate Candy's life even more. However Candy was always willing to play the hand that she was dealt. Candy baby daddy use to beat her with broom sticks and even left her baby girl on the bench at The City High School. That situation caused Candy to drop out of School at 9th Grade. Life was really hard for Candy. Candy Aunt Minnie stepped up and said she would take Candy and her baby girl in and they could live with her as long as possible. Candy was so excited about going to stay with her Aunt Minnie. Candy didn't know how much longer she could take her Grandma madness. Finally a stable place for her and her baby girl Candy thought to herself. Lauren was in and out of Candy's life going through hard times with one of her boyfriends and working. Davion was Lauren's 3rd child. Candy had no clue where her brother was. She often thought of Davion and hoped that he wasn't going through the things that she was going through. Living with her Aunt Minnie was really fun. Her Aunt Minnie use to write bad checks to buy food and they would stay up late at night watching movies and eating popcorn. Growing up Candy use to hate seeing a certain face. A face that still hunts Candy to this very day. She would cry all the time whenever she saw this person. Candy allowed this person situation to hunt her forever. At night she would wake up beside Ray in a cold sweat screaming crying help me. Ray would always comfort Candy when he was home. Candy never ever told anyone about her life or her family. How could she would anyone believe her? This face that hunted her though out the night. Was an All American face in everyone else eyes. Candy knew the truth and she paid a hell of a price for knowing it. Candy had so many skeletons in her closet. Candy was afraid to expose them to anyone. No one knew the real Candy but Candy and at times she looked in the mirror and wonder what type of person has she become? Would Candy allow the past to hunt her? From the married men she use to sleep with before she met Ray. To all the different dudes she had been with. To her baby girl that she had just one day left behind with her Aunt Minnie. All about the chicks that would spread Candy name in the streets telling lies about her. The many abortions that she had after she had her baby girl at the age of 13. Leaving her sterile not able to bare kids anymore. Candy knew that Ray wanted to be a Father. That was one thing she knew that he wanted and she couldn't give him a child. To the same sugar daddy that she had for the last 15 years. The real reason Candy had walked away from all her family even her baby girl. Candy was never ashamed of her past if she did it she would tell you. That was just the way Candy was. However Candy knew that everything wasn't meant to be told to everyone. Everyone in the streets just whispered about the things she had done instead of just asking her. Candy was thinking to herself could Ray handle my past? Would he walk away from me? Would he seek love and loyalty from someone else? Or would he be a standup guy and be there for her if she poured out her life story? Candy had so many questions and no answers as she thought to herself. Candy's life story was so crazy you would think it came out of a book. No one would have ever lived through everything Candy lived through and survive. Don't everyone have skeletons in their closet? Would Ray understand that Candy was doing all those different things with guys seeking love real love? Candy thought to herself I have Ray and I'm never ever letting go. As Candy thought about her life and everything that happen before she met Ray. Candy wondered if she ever told Ray would the nightmares stop.

Chapter 8: Candy and Ray...

Ray had caught Candy thinking about something as he entered the room. Candy was lost in her thoughts and wasn't even paying attention. Candy knew that Ray had slept when Sapphire however she would never ever bring it up to Ray. Candy would just sweep it under the rug that's how Candy always dealt with things in her life. Sweep everything up under the rug and try to forget. This time it wasn't as easy Candy loved Ray and would do anything for him including killing someone if she had to. Candy would never understand why Ray was stepping out sexing other chicks especially her friend Sapphire. Candy was hurting everything that Candy was trying to forget kept resurfacing in her brain. Life was getting harder and harder by the day. Ray had everything but everything meant nothing. The cars, the clothes, shopping sprees, exotic trips, and the home they shared meant nothing to Candy. Yes of course these things are nice. Candy thought to herself as she looked around.

Ray: Hi baby what are you up to?

Candy: Nothing just sitting here thinking about life and the things you have given me. I love you Rayshawn with everything in me. I just want you to know that I'm never ever leaving you. You will have to kill me that's the only way.

Ray: Looked at Candy as if she was CRAZY. What have I got myself into? Ray thought Ray loved Candy as well he just couldn't stop sexing other chicks. Ray wanted Candy to be his wife like and do others on the side. Ray already knew if Candy stepped out on him what he would do. He would not only beat the living hell out of her. He would kill her and make sure the police never ever finds her body. All that Candy knew about Ray and his operation. The kilos that Candy have seen the money. Ray knew in his head that Candy could cross him and Ray would be facing a life sentence mandatory in a Federal Penitentiary. Ray knew that Candy knew he had sex with Sapphire. Ray wanted Sapphire out the way. Ray hated the fact that Sapphire was always around. Ray knew that Sapphire wasn't shit and would fuck for nothing. Ray just prove a point to Candy. Never ever TRUST anyone especially a BITCH. Candy bent down and kissed Ray in the mouth. Candy told Ray my sentence with you never expires. She bent down a little more and sucked the cum out of Ray dick just to seal the deal. Ray took a shower got dressed and left the house.

.

Chapter 9: Candy meets her new friend,

Candy was sitting in the same spot on the bed after Ray left. Candy thought to herself I'm tired of everything I just wish I had something to ease my mind. Something to numb the pain of life Candy thought I met Ray and I felt my life would be better. Candy was feeling as if she was in too deep with Ray. She needed to tell Ray about her life everything that has happen. In the meantime Candy did the unthinkable. Candy got up under the king size bed, grab the baby wipe container smashed up some cocaine made a piled and snorted. Candy life was about to take a turn for the worst. What have I done Candy thought to herself? I have never done any hard drugs before besides drink and smoke a little weed here and there. OMG what have I just done? Wait I know I wanted to just ease the pain escape. Have sex with Ray and stay #1 in his eyes. Ray had sex with Sapphire for what reason? Candy thought to herself it has to be something more he wants I'm doing everything I can possible do or am I? Candy had to call Ray she was too high and couldn't think straight.

Ring, Ring, Ring,

Ray answered after what seem like forever to Candy.

Ray: Yo

Candy: I need you to come back home.

Ray: Why what's wrong?

Candy: I got into the container. Candy started to cry my heart is beating fast Ray I'm scared. Please come home hurry Candy said. I never felt this way before.

Ray: I'm on my way Ray said before hanging up the phone.

Ray knew that Candy would never be the same. Ray where are you Candy? Where are you Ray was yelling as he walked in? What have you done Candy? Ray started to cry why? Why? Why? Candy couldn't say nothing she was to high off the pure cocaine that was once stored in the baby wipe container.

Candy was stuck and she felt as if everything was moving in slow motion. She heard what Ray was saying however she wasn't listening. She was high and thirsty Ray made her sit in the recliner. Ray went outside still crying and called his friend. Ray was explaining the situation at the end of the conversation Ray said I will never ever be able to trust her anymore. Ray came back in and Candy was scared to say anything. Really she was high and horny just wanted to fuck and suck Ray's dick. Forget about life and everything else and just enjoy the moment with Ray. Candy knew that would never happen not under these conditions. Candy could taste Ray cum in her mouth and his package between her legs better yet her ass. Yea that would be best Candy thought to herself. Damn I'm high as fuck I shouldn't have never called Ray. By this time Candy was coming down off her first high and she needed more cocaine. Ray didn't say anything more he reached over and grab the back of Candy's head. Ray beat the shit out of Candy. Kicking her crying and saying you stupid bitch you will never be the same. So much was happening and running through Candy's mind. She felt as if she deserve everything that is happening to her. Candy felt as if she couldn't win with Ray. The more she tried to win the more she lost with Ray. It was a game of chess and Candy was the pawn every single time. Eventually after Ray stop beating the shit out of Candy. Ray left taking the baby wipe container with him. Candy was still horny, a little high and sore as hell from the ass beating she just endured. Candy fell asleep when she woke up she was sore and mad at herself. Candy didn't understand how a couple of lines of coke could change her life forever. She would later find out what Ray meant by she would never be the same. Cocaine is one of the most addictive drugs. Would Candy become an addict better known as a powder head in the streets?

Chapter 10: Rayshawn And Candy…

When Ray finally came back home he was upset. Candy and Ray talked about a couple of things most importantly her staying off cocaine and what made her get into his supply of cocaine. Candy lied for the first time with the straight face that she would stay off cocaine. Scared as hell of getting another ass beating if she told him the truth that she would prefer to be high than deal with his ass everyday he would beat her for sure there was no doubt in Candy's mind. Dealing with Ray was becoming harder and harder by the day between the beatings, having sex, cleaning and cooking staying alive became an everyday struggle. At times Candy thought Ray would kill her. Candy thought I should just speak up and ask him where he took that container of cocaine. After that long boring talk that Ray had by his self. Candy's body was in his presence. Her mind was on snorting some more lines of cocaine By Any Means and not letting him find out. She was thinking that was the best she has felt in a long time. Candy wanted more coke Ray went and took a hot shower. Ray likes to takes long shower when he isn't leaving the house anytime soon. Candy already knew that Ray was most likely out fucking some random chick because he was mad at her for getting into that coke. To her surprise when Ray got out the shower he left again and that was find with her. Candy went looking for her new found friend Cocaine. She was digging through clothes looking under the bed like the baby wipe container was still there. Candy was looking and wanted something residue at this point anything that looked like cocaine would do. With no luck she decided it was a lost cause for now that is. Candy stayed away from her new friend cocaine for a period of time. She always felt like the coke was calling her name Candy, Candy, Candy. Was the cocaine calling her name? Would she answer?

CHAPTER 11: Ray & Candy

Candy was still getting hit on kicked on and nutted in and on like she wasn't shit. Candy thought to herself she was going to stay her love was greater than ever. She not only needed Ray but wanted him. Her mind, heart and body was playing tricks on her. One thing that wasn't playing tricks on her was wanting some cocaine. RIGHT NOW I need some cocaine Candy thought to herself. Candy couldn't tell Ray even if he was the man with the kilos there was no way she would able be able to break that news to him. Rayshawn was so hard to deal with wanting to give him everything and all of her was so hard. When Candy said I LOVE YOU to Ray she meant just that. She was loyal, real and honest and all Candy qualities could later become a deadly trait. She was destined to be his WIFE and someone he could depend on forever. All Candy and Ray have been through one would think they were already husband and wife. No she was still just his girlfriend. If Ray ever hit rock bottom and lost everything including his freedom Candy was going to be there for him. This relationship was getting harder by the weeks, days let alone the hours Candy thought. Ray was a super hard to deal with no lie straight drink no chaser. A hard pill to swallow. Candy was still trying to stay off cocaine. Every time Candy did something wrong Ray would hit her. Anywhere his hand landed that's the part of her body that would hurt like hell the next day. Many people would wonder why she stayed with Ray. Its simple Candy was addicted to his smell, touch, sex and the coke. Things finally turned up a notch. Ray gave Candy permission to go and enroll in school. Candy thought to herself finally I can get out of the house. Candy had already obtain her High School Diploma through online courses behind Ray's back. Candy went and enrolled in The Community College. She was going to become a Registered Nurse (RN). She knew it was going to take a long time to finish up and a lot of student loans. However Candy wasn't going to give up no matter what. She had no friends and Ray had push her family away. Ray wanted Candy all to his self. Candy thought to herself finally a break I will only have to deal with Ray at night when I came home from College. Candy already had a plan in motion when Ray said go and enroll in The Community College she would take as many classes as possible and stay late all the time that way I won't have to be home and get ass beatings. I really hope Ray lets me finish Candy thought. Candy said a silent pray to GOD. Please GOD let Rayshawn let me finish and become a RN please GOD please. Thank you LORD as tears fell from Candy eyes. As she said Amen. Candy hoped that out of 7 days at least 4 of them would be good days with Ray. Hell at this point I am willing to take 3 days Candy thought. Candy was happy to get home and call Ray and let him know how the process went with College Enrollment. Everything was smooth sailing. Candy always felt like if she was able to finish College she could talk Ray into going legal. Of course Candy already knew that her happiness wasn't going to last long. When Ray came home he handed Candy a Nextel Cell Phone. You know one of the phones that your able to use like a walkie - talkie. She asked Ray what's going on. Ray stated since you want to be out of the house so bad and I'm willing to let you to go to The Community College now here goes your cell phone. I need to keep track of you Ray stated. That's just what Ray would do keep track of Candy she wouldn't and couldn't get a break from Ray. I can't wait until College start. Candy was beginning to get consumes with her own thoughts of killing Ray. He was taking her through so much she had to be strong and stay strong. There is no way I can get a MURDER CHARGE and have to do a LIFE SENTENCE Candy thought.

Chapter 12: Candy...

College finally started 3 weeks after enrollment. Gosh I'm so happy to get out of the house Candy thought as she drove to school. Candy had to wear a long sleeve turtle neck from fighting with Ray. Well getting her ass beat yet again it didn't make no sense. Candy couldn't miss the first day of school it was 102 degrees outside and she had to wear a long sleeve turtle neck trying to hide the damage Ray had done to her body and neck. The first day of school she met this chick name Tasha. She was pretty cool but lame Tasha was book smart. When Candy met Tasha she thought of her old bitch ass friend Sapphire. This time around she would be a friend to Tasha. However there was no way that Candy would ever disclose info about Ray. What he did or where they stayed nothing. Everything about Candy's personal life would stay just that way personal. Candy was determined to have one friend that Ray didn't know about. Life was getting hard and Candy was feeling very alone in this big ass world of millions and millions of people. Tasha was soft spoken and asked a lot of questions. Candy didn't like that at all she gave Tasha a little bit of her. Candy already know that you can't give everybody every detail about yourself and your life. Some people are out for their own personal gain. School was a wonderful choice Candy thought to herself as she held a small conversation with Tasha. The whole class of 24 receive their text books and rate of pay if they finish up the whole course and Graduated. We will be making 80,000 per year once we get our Career started. I can't wait I'm ready to start making my own money Candy thought to herself. Ray had everything and gave Candy everything however it's nothing like your own. Ray control everything from all the money he gave her to what she drove and when she would drive it. To the sex they had how long Candy would suck his dick and ride him. If they had anal sex, threesomes, when he felt like kicking her ass and punching her in the mouth literally. Ray control every single thing including but not limited to Candy's mind, body and soul. Candy had her own ML430 Mercedes Benz Truck that Ray had brought.

Ring, ring, ring

Candy already knew who it is was. Only one person had her number RAY. Excuse me Mr. Southland I have to step out and take this important call. Mr. Southland excuse Candy.

Candy: Hello hi Ray.

Ray: Where are you Candy?

Candy: I'm at the Community College I told you I had school today.

Ray: You need to come home right not and I mean right now.

Candy: What!!!!!!! Ray please just wait until class is over. It's over at 2pm please Ray Candy begged.

Ray: No I said now or you going to get your ass beat. Candy don't play with me you have 15mins to get home. Click Ray hung up.

Candy walked back in class. Excuse me Mr. Southland I need to be excused for the rest of the day. I have a family emergency. Mr. Southland excuse Candy but let her know that she would have to make up her work. Candy told Tasha that she would see her later and left in a hurry. There was no way she could give Tasha her cell phone number if she wanted to. Ray made that very clear that she isn't allowed to give anyone that number and he meant just that. Candy already knew if she did gave her number out would Ray would act a fool. On the way home Candy put some music on and pressed the gas running lights 15 minutes goes by very fast Candy thought as she looked down at her watch. 14 minutes later Candy pulled up in front of the house and rushed in the front door. Ray was sitting at the table he said sit down Candy we need to talk. Candy was thinking OMG what have I done now? The house is clean, his clothes are laid out, his food is ready in the microwave Candy did a mental note of everything that she was told to do before she left for class. Candy looked at Ray and set down in the chair across from him. Ray said Candy I'm happy that you're in

By Any Means.. Written By C. Janae

school and out of the house. Don't make me take you out of school for disobeying my every command. Ray said he needed her Candy to do everything he said do right when he said do it. Candy was thinking DAMN aren't I already marching to his beat like I'm in a fucking band. Ray went on to say I know you been wanting to get high. I know you have but BITCH if I ever find out your getting high off my kilos of cocaine. I'm going to fuck up you in the worst way. Candy looked at Ray scared to say anything. Candy just thought to herself oh Ray the shit you put me through every day and every night I'm going to get high with or without your permission. Ray told Candy I am putting my trust in you and I'm going to trust that your loyalty is with me and only me. She took a deep breath thinking just give me some cocaine please Ray. Those were her thoughts at this time Candy wasn't saying anything she was to afraid. Ray told Candy if you ever tell anyone about the things that go on in this house and what you have seen I will KILL you. As you know Candy I have ties with the Mexican Cartel and I can touch you without even touching you myself. Candy if you ever think about taking my money or anything from me and running. I will hunt you down and KILL you I will make you suffer a slow painful death. Even if you ever think about going to the Federal Agents on me and they put you in Protective Custody. I will find you Candy I will KILL you. Candy just set there thinking what the HELL have I got myself into? Head first at that I'm SCARED as hell Candy thought. Candy was locked in with Ray deeper than she would ever know. Candy thoughts were I might get my ass beat every other day I'm laced with nothing but the best of everything. I know for a fact that my stress and tears are going to pay off in the end at least she hope so. Ray told her to go and start weighing up 2 grams of cocaine he supplied the scale. To be honest with you her body was calling for a line but there was no way she could steal any of Ray cocaine or tell him. Candy just set there bagging up cocaine for the next 6 hours lost in her own thoughts. Thoughts about her life everything that she is going through with Ray. Really just thoughts of is she going to survive through all of this. A plan popped up in Candy's head I'm going to think of something I can't keep dealing with this ass beatings, sex life with Ray. I have to get out of this some type of way Candy thought to herself. I'm tired and my love, lust and out of fear I can't leave, I won't leave, I need to leave. What am I going to do Candy thought? She needed help getting away and when she really thought about everything she had no one to help her get away from Ray. Ray and Candy got done bagging up the cocaine. Ray went in the kitchen and turned on the stove. Candy stood back and watched Ray really meticulous. First Ray would run the cold water than he put some water in the pot with the baking soda adding the 2 grams of cocaine stirring it really good under the cold water until it got hard and it became an ounce of dope. An ounce is shaped like a cd you know the ones you listen to in your car. That's about the diagram of an ounce of dope. Ray did that all day long until he had about 70 ounces. Candy set there and watched just in case Ray ever left her. She would know how to get money and stay on top of everything with or without Ray. Candy wasn't going back to nothing. Candy bagged the ounces for wholesale feeling notorious just like Ray felt. As if he couldn't be touched by no one Federal Agents, Robbers, no one could touch Ray that's what he thought. Ray would soon find out that he could be touched. The smell of pure cocaine is so potent it was like a mixer of vinegar or something. Candy really can't explain the smell. She knew the smell when she smelled it that is all that mattered to her.

Chapter 13: Candy

The first time Candy got high off cocaine it was a feeling that she couldn't explain. All she knew she needed to get high and fast. The next day Candy went back to class. Her and Tasha hooked up she was asking Candy so many questions. Candy stated damn bitch do you ever get tired of asking me a MILLION questions? The one thing Tasha didn't know is that Candy hated to be asked questions. Especially about her personal life. There was no way Candy would let another bitch play her like her friend Sapphire did.

Mr. Southland, pulled out all the lessons for today. Candy was super excited to jump back into class. She had missed out on a lot, Mr. Southland graded the assignments Candy had an A+ on all of her assignments. Candy was really smart whenever she went to School. Even on the online classes she always made an A+ on every paper. No matter what was going on Candy always wanted to be smart and stay smart. Candy would read a lot of books on everything. From urban fiction, How to become a Publisher, Self – Improvement, Newspapers whatever type of books you could think of Candy would read. Candy knew for a fact that she would become someone of importance in this cruel world. What she didn't know was when she met Rayshawn B. Jones he would distract her every goal and dream in life. Ray messed up some parts of my life Candy thought to herself. Everyday became harder and harder. Things were looking up in school anyways. Candy spoke with Tasha before school let out. Tasha was saying something about going to a club. Candy just ignored everything that Tasha was talking about. Candy already knew that Ray wasn't going to let her go anywhere that was out point blink period. School, home and the grocery store sometimes the mall. Oh yea and the bathroom before and after sex and see what damage Ray had done after he beat the shit out of her. Going out with some random chick that was OUT. Candy was shocked that Ray let her out the house to go to school. Life was CRAZY with a CAPTIAL C. When Candy finally made it home Ray wasn't there. She took a relaxing bubble bath and fixed herself a stiff shot of Remy Martell. She needed to enjoy this time by herself. At least to try and relax in her bubbles and get her thoughts together. About 3 more shots and after taking that long hot bubble bath Candy was ready for some hardcore sex. She could feel her pussy getting wet that was weird been that Ray and Candy fought all the time. All in all she was dripping wet with cum and Ray wasn't even home yet.

Imagine that......

Chapter 14: Ray and Candy

Candy ended up falling asleep horny around 7pm. She awoke at 3am looking around for Ray. Of course Ray was nowhere to be found he wasn't even home. That was totally weird to Candy Ray always came home around 11pm. She called and text Ray with no luck Candy was worried only because she knew what type of work Ray was doing. Where is he? Is he locked up dead or what? Candy thought to herself.

Ray was moving major dope and this is the first time Candy felt scared. She didn't know where Ray was. Candy sat up replaying every situation that had happen and what is happening now. The long talks the fights and everything that has happen since the first day she talked to Ray. Would she only have memoires of Ray left?

Ray finally called about an hour later.

Ring, Ring, Ring

Candy: Hello Ray where are you?

Ray: What are you doing up?

Candy: I rolled over in the bed I didn't see you. I walked around the house and you haven't been home. Where are you Ray?

Ray: I'm out and about I'm good don't question me Ray told Candy.

Candy: Wait who are you with Ray?

Ray: Didn't I say don't question me Candy. When I get home I'm going to beat the shit out of you. So be waiting for my foot to go in your ass. Ray clicked the phone in Candy's ear.

Candy thought to herself that conversation didn't go to good. She had set there worrying about him and now I have to get my ass beat. Damn Candy set there crying thinking to herself I can't win for losing with Ray. She figured she might as well get up and take some more shots of Remy Martell matter of fact she will just drink the whole damn bottle. Reality was Candy really wish she had some cocaine to deal with this shit. This life is becoming too much to deal with sober Candy said out loud to herself. It's going on 5am I'm up drinking I have to get my ass beat for worrying about his black ass. Class starts at 7am she set there looking stupid waiting.

5:45am she heard the key in the door.

DAMN, DAMN, DAMN, DAMN, DAMN, Candy thought to herself. Here we go again and I'm kicking myself before he even starts to kick me. All I could think about is I won't be going to school in the morning.

Ray: Come here Candy now.

Candy: I'm coming Ray.

Ray: Now Candy right now.

Yes Ray I'm sorry for asking you who you were with. Before she could finish the sentence Ray was kicking her punching her and chocking the life out of Candy. Ray even spit dead in her face she didn't even try to fight back. Candy just laid there at this point and every point before Candy wanted to give up and die. Something in Candy kept fighting some little voice in Candy kept saying don't give up hold on things are going to get better. She whispered asking the voice when? When will things get better? Ray kept kicking her Candy balled up and cried out please Ray Please stop please I'm sorry. Candy had to try and stay strong. She had so many scars on her face, neck, whole body you would have thought she was in World War #2. This is my second and last boyfriend Candy thought to herself. Her thoughts were she couldn't tell Ray that he has ruin everything for every other dude that would ever approach her. Candy end up missing the next 3 days of school. She need to go to the hospital what was she going to tell them without getting Ray in trouble. It seems like Ray and school was Candy's only concern in the world. She could worry about everything even herself later on in life. That's if she lived through everything Ray was taking her through.

She would deal with her pain, thoughts, and scars later on. When Candy was out of school for 3 days she bagged and delivered cocaine for Ray. This was all his idea Candy thought she knew nothing about cooking dope, bagging dope or delivering dope before she met Ray. One thing Ray forgot to tell her is if she ever got caught with his product, money or with all this cocaine boxes and boxes of baking soda and the Pyrex 1.5 pots in their house. They were both going to a Federal Penitentiary for a very long time. Ray never mention that to Candy. Candy already knew that she had to take Ray back his money sometimes more than $50,000 dollars. Candy was taking a chance no risk riding with all that cocaine and money. Ray had sent her straight into the lion's den and she was the meat. Candy wanted to steal the money and cocaine from Ray. However, there was no way she would ever lie, cheat or steal from Ray. Even if the thought crossed her mind that was just out. After all the things Ray had put her through up to this point Candy wanted Ray to trust her and know that no matter what happens in life he could always count on her. Candy thought to herself that she would never betray Ray. Or would she?

Chapter 15: Candy And Ray

Candy wished she had her best friend Diamond. She knew she couldn't call Diamond when Candy met Ray he let it be known that he wanted her to his self. Candy had to cut everyone off. Diamond and Candy were best friends for 15 years. The hardest thing in the world was leaving Diamond behind. Diamond had been there through everything. Growing up Diamond didn't like Candy because she wore beads with braids in her hair. Once they both started talking they fell in love with one another and became best friends. Diamond would always come and rescue Candy out of some trouble she had gotten herself in. Even though Diamond life was totally different than Candy's. Diamond never looked down on Candy and always prayed for Candy and whatever it was she was going through. Candy miss her so much and the thoughts of Diamond brought tears to her eyes. Diamond was Candy backbone that's before she met Ray. Diamond was the type of friend that would walk 1,000 miles with Candy. Candy hoped and prayed that Diamond would still be the same person. Whenever she got in contact with Diamond. Candy always had a habit of knocking on the door of the house so Ray would know that she was coming in. She guess Ray wasn't home. Glad Candy thought I can get a break. Candy entered the room and Ray was sleeping in the bed. She hurried up and walked back out of the room. Praying that today would be a good day. Candy went in the kitchen to fix her something to eat. Sat down to eat took a bite. Candy was sitting there quite trying not to wake up Ray. Her back was turned away from the room door. Candy was deep in thought the next thing she knew. Ray hands were around her neck and she was choking on her food. Ray was choking her without saying anything. Candy was crying that's all she could do when she was about to take her last breath Ray let her go. She stared to vomit all over the place she throw up so much blood was coming out of her eyes. After about 45 minutes Candy was able to pull herself together. Ray what have I done now? Candy asked. Ray said I looked through your Nextel and seen where Tasha had giving you her number. Candy went through her mental index I could have sworn I didn't store her number in my phone. I knew the rules and I always stayed on my tippy toes Candy thought to herself. I was trying not to break any of Ray rules that was impossible everyday Ray would come up with more rules. Candy was thinking what other way would Ray have Tasha number? Ray said Tasha number out loud all seven digits. Did he know her? There was no way he could have known Tasha or was there? Candy couldn't wait until the next day of class. She felt crazy like a caged animal with no water and no food. In an Arizona Desert heat exhaustion was getting the best of Candy that's how she felt. Candy could barely hold her tears in she was just crying and crying.

She needed someone anyone to talk to, lean on just someone to tell her that things would get better. Pray with her and just allow her to cry on their shoulder. Candy had no one and that's when reality hit her like a ton of bricks. Candy needed some motivation to get through school and last but not least some real genuine love. When Candy thought about everyone that once cared about her. Her Aunt Minnie and her Best friend Diamond she realized that only two people in the world loved her and she allowed Ray to push them away. Ray came into her life and demanded her full attention, all her love, her body, her mind, her heart Candy at times felt possessed. Candy would kill for Ray if he said so. She would suck his dick after getting beat in the mouth. Ray beat her whenever he felt like it. Whenever he got out of line with one of those whores in the streets. He would come home and make Candy feel as she was the cause. In reality Candy made Ray a better man all in all. At the time Ray wanted to be in the streets get money fuck different hoes and keep Candy held in the house as his hostage and he wasn't negotiating with anyone. Candy met Ray every need she was on beck and call putting her wants and needs on hold for Ray. Many people would call Candy stupid she was madly in love with Ray. Candy never ever cared about what anyone thought about her and Ray. Even if Candy lost herself dealing with Ray that was a price that she would be willing to pay later on in life if it came down to that. Candy really hope that Ray would change his ways soon. Candy was willing to let go of her hopes, dreams, sanity and dignity for Ray. She was willing to stand for nothing and fall for anything for Ray. If Ray brought home AIDS Candy would still accept Ray. If he brought home a baby she would accept that as well. However, there was one thing that Ray wasn't going to do to Candy and she would sit back and watch it happen and do nothing. Hell no Candy thought to herself. I will bury him first and that is on everything well everything that she had left anyways. That wasn't much of nothing with all those jumbled up thoughts in her head she fell asleep. Candy jumped her heart was beating fast she didn't even look for Ray. Its 6:00am class starts soon Candy hurried up and jumped in the shower, brush her teeth, brush her little bit of hair that she had left. Ray had pulled out all her pretty black hair that she once had. Candy went outside to leave for school and her truck was gone. What the fuck? Candy yelled out loud Ray knows I have to go to school. Why would he take the truck? Candy was furious mad as hell at Ray. She really enjoyed getting out of the house and Ray knew that. He always have to fuck something up Candy thought. Damn you Ray I'm starting to hate you fuck this love shit. It's not getting me anywhere. Candy went in the house and started to cry and she cried for everything. She cried so much her eyes were closed shut. She look as if she had been beat up by 10 people at one time. Candy realized once again that she couldn't call the 2 people that she knew loved her. If it wasn't Ray kicking her ass reality was beating the hell out of her. Ray and I stayed in this small City Called Press more. Candy thought she could walk to school. However, it was 30 minutes in a car so imagine how long it would take to walk. She undressed and laid in bed at a time like this Candy just wish she was dead. She wish had a gun to kill herself she felt like a worthless piece of shit. If this is the best that life has to offer. I can lay down right here and die Candy thought to herself. She went back to thinking the first time she got high off of cocaine. Candy felt nothing no ounce of pain the first time she snorted those lines. Fuck it I'm going to get me some cocaine fuck Ray, fuck love, fuck my life, fuck everything I'm getting high. Candy knew that once she was high she would forget everything for a minute anyways. If she had to walk to get some cocaine that is what she would have to do. Shit if I'm going to live like this I'm going to do it high the whole time. Ray is just going to beat the shit out of me anyways. I might as well be high if I have to suck his small ass dick I will do it high. If I have to do anal with no lubrication I will do it high. I'm going to deal with his ass high. I allowed STUPID ass Ray to push the two people that cared about me away. Candy was talking to herself out loud. Happy Ray isn't home I haven't got my cocaine yet Candy said….

Chapter 16: Candy, Ray, Tasha and Chris

I called Tasha I remember her number that's how I knew that I never stored it in my Nextel. I asked Tasha to come and get me from 190th street that was about 20 blocks from Ray and I house. I never ever wanted her to know where I lived with Ray. I walked down to 190th street and Tasha pulled up. Tasha drove a black Kia spectra with 18in rims and music. Tasha had a cute little car that some old dude had brought for her brand new off the lot. This bitch isn't cute at all Candy thought and hell no I'm not a hater. Tasha did have a nice body but she always had an odor about herself. I asked Tasha could I borrow $100.00 dollars I knew that I wasn't going to pay the bitch back. How the fuck did Ray know her number? I also knew that Tasha was a bitch and would tell Ray my every move I made. I was going to get me some cocaine and I didn't care who knew what I was going to do. I never did make it school to confront this bitch as to how Ray got her number. I refuse to say anything to her now I'll just play it cool I know this funky odor bitch is going to slip. Tasha and I rode to the projects called The Park. I knew this one dude name Chris he sold coke he was a major player in the game as well. Chris wasn't as big as Ray in the kilo game however he moved weight. Chris was cool as ever I knew him a long time before I ever met Ray. I met Chris back in the 1990's Candy was telling Tasha. Tasha was just laughing talking about for real girl. How he look? Tasha bitch Chris has gold teeth of course he likes Cadillac's cars and he is a get money nigga by any means. Chris is thick and I heard through the grapevine he has some good dick. I never mess with him before I just heard he be moving cocaine before I met Ray Candy told Tasha. Candy asked Tasha to go to the door for her. Tasha dumb ass left her phone. Candy went through her phone and what she seen would be a surprise to her. Candy seen text messages from Ray to Tasha. Tasha had been in Candy's and Ray house. Candy thought to herself how? When? Where was I? When Ray was doing all this with Tasha? No this can't be not to Candy knowledge Ray and Tasha were creeping behind her back. Candy went to thinking CRAZY she wanted to kill Tasha. Now Candy knew for a fact that Tasha was going to tell Ray everything that is happening. All about Chris and everything else. SLIMY FUNKY BODY BITCH Candy said out loud sitting in Tasha car. No wonder how Ray knew this BITCH number. Ray was fucking this bitch the whole time. I knew that I never stored this bitch number in my phone I'm not that crazy Candy said to herself. Candy thought to herself I knew not to befriend anyone I knew that. Candy was hot and heated I still want my cocaine I wish this bitch come on with my shit. With those thoughts Candy laid Tasha phone back down. Once again this shit is happening Ray can't control his little ass dick. I bet that bitch was disappointed. I love Ray for Ray not his sex game truth is I never ever had an orgasm. I make myself nut dumb ass bitches going to learn about fucking with Ray. Tasha finally came back with the cocaine all smiling and shit. Most likely ready to call Ray and let him know where I had been. Candy guess the saying was true when you go looking for something you find it. She was looking straight ahead pissed to the max. Candy thought these simple minded dumb bitch ass hoes are going to learn not to cross me. I'm Ray WIFE and I am not going anywhere. I said my sentence is LIFE rather it be my life or Ray life. One of us are going to DIE before I ever let go. With that thought Candy smiled thinking that's if we aren't already dying SLOWLY that is…

Chapter 17: Candy And Tasha

Tasha gave Candy the bag of cocaine. Candy knew that Chris would look out for her he always did on the cocaine. Chris knew Candy whole story Candy didn't know that Chris knew everything she had been through and was going through. Chris was well connected in the streets. Candy went to thinking I'm scared to leave Ray. She was scared of Ray actions and what he would do to her if he even knew that Candy was thinking about leaving him. Candy put the straw in the bag and inhaled deep. Shit I been waiting on this shit Candy said out loud as the cocaine hit her and she lean her head back on the head rest. Tasha hoe take me home I'm sure you already know where I stay with Ray. Tasha looked at Candy like she was CRAZY. No bitch I'm not CRAZY at all. I went through your phone you dumb ass bitch I know you have been fucking Ray in our home. I'm going to tell you like I told Ray. Somebody will DIE before I leave and I mean that. So if you continue to cross me just know Tasha that you already signed a death certificate when you laid your funky ass down with him. However I will be the Notary if you keep fucking with Ray. Tasha just kept looking at Candy. Bitch don't watch me watch the road Candy said. Tasha couldn't say anything she knew she was ready to get Candy's CRAZY ass out her car. Oh and why you at it when sucking Ray's dick just know that your jaws will be hurting for nothing. And your stinky ass pussy will be getting wet for nothing. You would have been better off playing in your own pussy. You remind me of Sapphire I am sure Ray told you all about her. How he fucked her fed her lies and she fell for the bullshit just as you have done. Silly rabbit bang bitch I have the gun and I will re-load it. Tasha arrived at the house she knew exactly where it was located. Truth was Tasha was falling for Ray after Candy said something to her she is not too sure if she should deal with Ray anymore. Candy jumped out the car with her cocaine and straw. Went in the house and waited on Ray. Tonight were going to fight until I can't fight no more. Ray has me totally fucked up Candy thought. This is the second time Ray has slept with someone that I knew. Not including the bitches I don't know. The whole City will be dead if he don't stop with his dumb ass. Out here tricking with these off brand random ass bitches. The more Candy thought about it the madder and madder she got. The minute Ray bring his ass home I'm going in on him. Candy grab the cocaine and before she knew it the whole bag was gone 6 grams of cocaine was gone. She was mad as hell and ready. Candy squatted behind the door with a bat. Soon as Ray entered with his key she hit him in the head. Kicked him in the mouth beat him with the bat. She was yelling you want to fuck these bitches in the street? What Ray I'm not good enough for you? What more do you fucking want from me? I gave up the only two people I know for your black hateful woman beating small dick ass. And this is how you repay me. Blood was coming from Ray head. Candy couldn't stand the sight of seeing Ray hurt. She stop hitting Ray with the bat and went to where he was laying. Ray I'm so sorry Candy said I'm sorry. Unlike Ray when he beat Candy and blood was drawn he didn't feel sorry. Candy always was soft for Ray and he knew that and used that to his advantage. I don't know if the cocaine is talking to me Candy thought I'm so high and horny. Kicking Ray's ass made Candy horny as hell. Ray never did get a hit or kick in this time. Candy finally was winning. Later on she would realize she may have won one but that would be the only one.

Chapter 18: Candy And Ray

As they laid in the bed. Ray was hurting and candy was enjoying every minute of the look of pain on Ray's face. From that bat beating she gave him. Ray looked up and said Candy I'm sorry. Candy looked down and said Ray you will be sorry for everything you have done to me later on in life. Ray one thing about me is I'm not here to play or be played by you. Your ways are no good for either one of us. You're out here fucking these bitches and those bitches be fucking other niggas. Than you come home and demand sex head and ass from me. Tell me Ray what's the point of me being here? Why am I here held hostage in this house? This is not fair Ray what do you want from me? I give you everything and everything is not enough. Candy said one of these days Ray you will find out the real me. You will see one of these days. My nose is bleeding I have to get some tissue. Ray already knew what that meant Candy had gotten some cocaine. From someone Ray would soon find out who. Little did Candy know Ray had sent Tasha to spy on her in class. Ray and Tasha have been fucking long before Candy even came along. Ray told Candy you can call and withdraw from school. Since one of these days I will find out the real you. Candy looked at Ray and said ok fine with me. Reality was Candy was hurt and wanted to cry well get high anyways. Ray is taking my dream away from me Candy thought as she dialed the school number. Candy would not be a Registered Nurse on Ray's watch. This bitch think I'm going to allow her to get a Degree and leave me she has another thing coming thought Ray. Ray wanted to get up and leave however he was stuck in bed from that bat beating. Ray would have to wait to find out everything that went on from Tasha. Ray didn't really like Tasha however she was always willing to do anything and everything that Ray said with no limits. Just like Candy I have these two bitches trained like dogs Ray thought. Little did Ray know Candy was already plotting on his ass. As for Tasha Candy thought in due time in due time. Her bitch ass will pay if I have to die trying to get revenge on these two. Candy always knew to act dumb when needed to act dumb. Play crazy and of course act deaf. Candy learned from her hard life to talk less and listen more. Watch a person real close and you will find out everything you need to know from that person. A person will always show their true colors.

Candy would never ever show her hand or what she really knew or would she?

Chapter 19: Candy And Ray

I have to get myself together and shake this habit. Damn I love getting high everything is gone all the pain. I can block Ray ass out and I love this shit. Candy thought to herself to her surprise she didn't even have any cocaine left. Damn she thought Ray was still laying around the house. His ass needs to leave. Candy had already peeped where Ray kept the cocaine. She would have to just get into the kilos and hope that Ray wouldn't find out some was missing. Candy took a shower and went in the room. Hey baby are you going somewhere today? Yea soon as I feel a little better you did beat the shit out of me last night. Candy didn't say anything she was just ready for his ass to go. Well what would you like to wear today? I'm going to go ahead and get it out for you. Damn Ray said I feel as if you're kicking me out of my own house. No not really Ray I'm kind of tired she lied. About an hour later Ray got up took a shower and left. Candy jumped up and went to the safe underneath the carpet. Candy had to move the king size bed. The Oriental rug and find out exactly where the main rug was cut. Jackpot Candy thought as she located the spot. Yes she thought as she open the safe up. Ray only used the same four numbers to everything that he had. His password to his phone. The safe the accounts that he thought Candy had no clue about. Candy entered the numbers 6572 click the safe unlocked. Candy grab the kilos out and unwrapped it. She knew that is was pure it was still in the brick form. Candy went to the kitchen with the kilo of cocaine and found a brand new razor. She cut off a chuck which weighted 4 grams when she put it on the scale. Candy already knew that she couldn't add baking soda to the kilo to make up for the grams that she had just cut. She just put the kilo back in the safe locked it. Place the main rug back the Oriental rug and moved the king size bed back in place. Ray would find out she thought to herself. Oh well by than I will be good and high and the grams of cocaine will be all gone. She knew she was going to get her ass beat real decent for stealing his cocaine. Oh well she thought to herself oh fucking well. All that he has done he can take all this shit and just give me a kilo of cocaine and allow me to over dose. I'm sick of his ass that was Candy's motivation to keep doing what she was doing. However, that same motivation she already knew would cost her. Candy went back down stairs and cut the gram up. This time she made line after line of cocaine. Long lines and short lines. She always had a package of straws in the house she cut her a straw. Bent down and inhaled the lines of cocaine in her nose. Damn this is some good ass cocaine Candy thought. Shit I have to shit that was something that she hated about cocaine. It always made her shit once she used the bathroom and took a long hot shower. She was ready for some hardcore sex. Sucking Ray dick hours at a time. Why her pussy just dripped with her cum. She actually loved sucking Ray's dick. Ray had already told her that she had the best head in American. Candy just laughed at the thought. After getting out the shower she was drying off when she heard Ray in the living room talking on the phone. Shit she thought I left the cocaine on the kitchen counter. She rushed down to the kitchen naked sliding past Ray unnoticed. Just as she was finishing wrapping up her cocaine she had stolen. Ray walked in Candy was real slick with her hands, She had put the wrapped cocaine in her pussy. Candy bent over and kiss Ray she was higher than a kite damn Ray said.

What's good?

She asked you already know my mouth is horny.

Where is he at?

Ray already knew that what she was talking about. Mr. is what Ray called his dick.

Where is Mr.? Candy asked. She looked away for one minute when she turned around Ray was standing there with Mr. in his hands. Candy got on her knees and Ray came in 30 seconds flat less than a minute. She swallowed his babies without hesitation. Damn she looked down on the floor and there was blood. She manage to wipe the blood with the bottom of her feet. Candy got up and went to the bathroom. Damn I need more cocaine she thought. My nose is stopped up and bleeding I have to get this coke in my nose some kind of way she thought. With those thoughts she blow and blow until all the blood was out her nose and it wasn't stopped up anymore. She grab the wrapped cocaine out her pussy and put the cocaine in her nose chewing the bag and all. She knew when she chewed the bag or wiped the cocaine around in her mouth that her mouth would be numb. Damn she thought and started playing in her pussy even though she had Ray downstairs. Sometimes Ray sex was just good when she was high off cocaine Ray sex was WONDERFUL GREAT. Right now she would prefer touching herself. As Candy thought about Sapphire and Tasha fucking Ray thinking they were about to get a pussy full she knew they were both disappointed when he pulled out that small short ass dick he has. Candy laughed as she reached her orgasm. She held a card that no one knew about that was going to change everyone life that was willing to cross her. They thought Candy would be the fool sit back and watch them play her.

Chapter 20: Ray And Candy

I have to get that kilo of cocaine sold Ray thought to his self. He had sent Candy out shopping. He thought she has been doing everything really well I haven't put my foot in her ass in a long time he thought. My wife is finally getting it. Ray was smiling at the thought of her marching to his every beat. Ray always thought as Candy as a doormat. Someone he would just walk over all the time and she would be dumb and come running back to him. Little did Ray know and would soon find out. She was far from dumb. When Ray was sending her out shopping Candy was banking half of the money that Ray was giving her. She knew that everything that sounded good was really not that good. She knew that Ray would one day try to leave her for one of these pussy hoes and she would need that money to hire a Lawyer once she got hit with a murder charge for killing Ray ass. Candy was making a deposit at the Grade Bank and Trust. Just as Ray was moving the king size bed. The Oriental Rug and went straight to his safe. As he was entering his code the bank teller was telling Candy her balance. Ms. Cane your balance is $450,000 dollars would you like to withdraw any money today? The teller asked Candy no thank you. This bitch Ray thought I am going to beat the fuck out of this bitch. He already knew that his kilo of cocaine had been mess with. Ray knew those kilos and grams like the back of his hand. Ray dreamed about kilos, grams, ounces and money. Why Candy had nightmares. 30 minutes later she walks in the house. Ray I'm home I brought you something Candy had forgot about the 4 grams of cocaine she had stolen from Ray. Before she knew it Ray was on her chocking, kicking, and punching her in the mouth. Damn he must have looked in the safe Candy thought to herself as she felt her front teeth come out. I knew this was going to happen and this is a price that I will have to pay. If I would have known he was going to go into the safe today. I would have went by the spot and seen Chris. Of course this is going to be the worst ass beating. Ray didn't stop beating her until she had passed out and he was still beating her and foaming at the mouth like a dog with rabies. When she woke up in the hospital she had broken teeth, a broken wrist, both of her eyes were swell shut and the Doctors had her neck in a brace. Candy couldn't move all she could do was lay there in pain. Thinking that was a good high nothing like the high she first got from the first cocaine she ever snorted. That would become an issue within itself that Candy would soon figure out she would never get or be as high as she was the first time she snorted those lines of coke. She would soon find out she was chasing a high that would never get caught again. In the meantime she had to get out of this hospital bed. All she could remember was her walking in the house and Ray beating her.

She knew she had went into the safe with the cocaine it. Candy was thinking I hope Ray isn't here. Just when that thought crossed her mind Ray was standing over her. Looking like the devil he bent down to her ear and whispered bitch I told you not to ever steal from me. I knew you was getting high again. Your dumb ass just couldn't stay away from the cocaine. She was force to listen to Ray and everything he had to say. She couldn't move talk or nothing, Ray said what bitch you thought I wouldn't find out you got into my safe? Did you really think I wouldn't know how my product was wrapped? If you ever tell anyone what I did to you Candy I will kill you. If you ever steal from me again I will kill you. When Ray got done talking he set back down. A tear fell out of Candy's eye. She thought you might as well kill me that's if I don't kill you first. Dr. Wan, walked in with Candy's chart as he looked over to the only person in the room. Ray stood up hi. Dr. Wan, asked Ray what happen to her? Ray said he came home and found her beat up in the front yard. You don't know what happen to her. Dr. Wan, already knew that Ray had done this to Candy. Dr. Wan, was a Doctor for over 15 years. He has seen many cases like this however, Candy's case was the worst. Dr. Wan, thought how could he beat her up like this? Just as Dr. Wan, was in his thoughts beep, beep, beep, beep, Candy's monitors were going off. Dr. Wan, press the button and the nurses came running.

They told Ray you have to leave now. Right now you have to get out of this room. She is dying her heart is failing her. Dr. Wan, was yelling out all kinds of codes code blue, code red bring the needles insert that morphine in her iv for pain. We have to get her awoke or she will have permanent brain damage. Hurry Dr. wan, was yelling. Dr. Wan, looked at Candy as she could have been his child. Why Candy was unconscious she heard the voice again. You can't give up you have to wake up Candy. You have a purpose in life you have to find it. Dr. Wan and his nurses finally got Candy heart beating and she was awake again looking around. All the nurses left out and Dr. Wan spoke to her you had all of us scared just than young lady. I want you to know that I know what happen to you. I know that your boyfriend did this to you. I don't know the whole story I do know for a fact that he beat you like this. I know that you can't talk Dr. Wan, told Candy. I don't think if you could talk you would tell me the truth anyways. Candy listen to me you have to get out you have to leave him. He is no good for you. I know he is a major player in the game. I've seen his type a million times you have to find your way baby girl and I will be praying for you. With that said Dr. Wan got up and walked away. Candy fell asleep with those thoughts Dr. Wan will be praying for me.

Chapter 21: Dr. Wan & Candy

Dr. Wan looked around he didn't see Ray anywhere. Dr. Wan spoke in a low tone to his head nurse. I really believe in my heart that Ray did this to her. Protocol is I have to call the police and make a report. Dr. Wan, was finishing his last words. Ray walked up on them. Ray said with a straight face a report what type of report? Dr. Wan, was a fast thinker. I have to review Candy's report stated Dr. Wan, as he walked away. Dr. Wan, hated the sight of Ray. It always amaze Dr. Wan, how a person can have so many personalities switching back and forward. Dr. Wan, was used to seeing this type of Domestic Violence just not a case this bad. With those thoughts Dr. Wan, picked up the phone and called 911

Ring, Ring, Ring

Dispatcher: Fence Police Department

yes I'm Dr. Author Wan I would like to report a domestic abuse case. The Patient name is Candy Cane last name Cane. I believe her boyfriend Ray' Shawn B. Jones.

Dispatcher: we will get an officer out to the Hospital. Is the attacker located in the hospital?

Dr. Wan: Yes he is in Candy's room at her bedside. And if doesn't look as if he is leaving stated Dr. Wan.

Dispatcher: Dr. Wan, the Officers are on their way to you.

The dispatcher and Dr. Wan hung up.

Dr. Wan, thought where is Candy family he wondered if she would tell on Ray. Dr. Wan, went on with his shift noting that he would come back to room #403 and check on Candy.

Candy woke up about 6 hours later. Dr. Wan, had been to check on her about 7 times he was really concerned about

Candy. Every time Dr. Wan, would check on her Ray was there. It was like Ray was glued to the bed that's how much he was there Dr. Wan, thought. Ray got up and walked over to Candy after Dr. Wan left. Ray whispered in Candy's ear. BITCH!!!!!! I will kill you if you tell on me. You think this was an ass beating this is nothing. If I go to jail behind this people you thought cared about you won't even be able to notice you. Now try me BITCH!!!!!!! Ray knew that Dr. Wan had called the police on him. Ray could feel it in his bones. That Dr. Wan, was a little to concern about Candy. As Ray finish the last sentence you better not forget what I said I don't give a damn how much medicine they pump in you. How much Dr. Wan show concern I'll KILL YOU!!!!! With that said Ray walked away. A tear fell out of candy's right eye as she thought of losing her life. This was the first time in a long time she prayed to God. After she met Ray she stop praying she knew that Ray was nothing but the DEVIL himself. Beep, Beep, Beep Dr. Wan, and the nurses was running in Candy heart was failing her once again. Ray already knew the routine he was walking slowly as the Doctor and nurses was running pass. Yet again they got Candy stabilize just as they were finishing up Agent. Price walked in the room. He spoke softly to Dr. Wan. Dr. Wan, told Agent. Price you don't have much time until the Jones boy comes back. Agent. Price walked over taking out a sheet of paper. Agent. Price said candy I need you to confirm that Rayshawn your live in boyfriend did this to you. Candy please we can put him in jail your beat up pretty bad. Candy held up her hand as Agent. Price gave her a pen. Candy wrote I can't and she put the pen down. Just as Agent. Price was moving the paper and pen away. Ray walked in speaking to Agent. Price. Agent. Price didn't speak back to Ray. Ray seen that Candy was up and walked over and kissed her on the lips. Hey baby how are you feeling? Candy still couldn't speak. Agent. Price seen the look that was in Candy's eyes a million times. Scared, nervous the look of hate and fear. As Agent. Price gathered his things he turn and said if you have any information on who did this to you Candy. Give me a call and he handed Ray a business card. Ray said oh we won't be needed that and tore the card up in many pieces right in Agent. Price face.

Agent. Price, looked up in Ray's eyes. Ray was drunk and high and that made Agent. Price even more upset. Agent. Price was going to get Rayshawn B. Jones. He thought to himself. How could someone do someone like this? And beat them up so bad like this? Where is her family Agent. Price thought?

Chapter 22: Chris And Lil J

Chris was wondering why he hasn't heard from Candy. Chris really liked Candy even though she was with Ray. Chris called up his main runner that goes by the name Lil J, to find out what was going on with Candy. Ray was known throughout the City and of course everyone knew that Candy was Ray's wife {Main chick}. Lil J, was very handsome he stood at 5'9 hand a nice set of lips. You know those type of lips like that rapper L.L Cool J. Lil J, has 5 open face gold teeth a low fade and he had a silly baby mama name Chanel. That bitch Chanel was a looney case. Chanel shared a home with Lil J and laid beside him whenever he decided to come home. Chanel thought she was on top until she found out the truth about her position. Lil J, came into the room. What's up bro? Lil J asked. Hey I need you to find out what's going on with that chick name Candy. You know the one that is messing with that nigga Ray. Candy came through and spoke with me about some coke. She gets high on the low and you know I knew of her before she hooked up with Ray Stated Chris. Candy comes off very Mysterious. It's something about her that I'm attracted to Chris told Lil J. Candy came through here with some chick name Tasha. Candy always calls me and whispering in the phone I haven't heard from her in about 3 months. I'm worried about her bro. Lil J, could see the look of concern in Chris face. Damn bro you really like the chick don't you? Chris just laughed a little. Chris told Lil J find out what you can and get back with me as soon as possible. With that said Lil J with straight to the worst projects in the City called the Pork and Pork projects. Lil J knew just who had to go to he was going to Prada's house. Dressed in a white and red True Religion outfit with some white and red J's on. Lil J jumped out his Audi Q7 Truck sitting on some Forgatio 30 inch rims. He was looking real handsome all the hood chicks wanted a piece of Lil J. and they would do whatever to get a piece. Even if it was nothing but a piece not even ½ of a piece. Just a little taste and I mean a little the chicks in the hood would sell their soul to fuck a rich nigga. Well a nigga they thought was rich but Lil J. was really just a runner. Chris and Lil J were two different types of dudes. Chris was more of the stick around the house type and get money major money. Lil J. wanted to be on every scene faking like he was a big time baller. Chris, really cared for Lil J. so he put him on and made sure he was straight.

Don't get me wrong Chris had clothes with tags and shoes still in the box. Chris, just wasn't big on impressing chicks that wouldn't matter in the end. However, Lil J was into impressing everyone and I mean everyone. Lil J, was walking up Prada house in the Pork and Pork Projects. Prada was a whore. Prada had fucked the whole Pork and Pork Projects even the girls, daddies and the little boys. I mean literally the whole Pork and Pork Projects. Getting this information would be easy Lil J. thought. Lil J. knew that Prada got high and that was her weakness. Lil J. would give her 2 grams of stepped on cocaine. That was once fish scale coke in other words pure cocaine. Prada mouth would run like diarrhea once she hit that cocaine. Prada was so gone she would tell on her damn self for some cocaine. One thing about Prada what she said was 100% TRUE. Prada stood about 4'2 she was thick about 2 years ago. Before she met some dude that got her hooked on cocaine. Now she is thin with dark circles around her eyes and she has short hair. One good thing about Prada is she didn't have any kids. Lil J, knocked on #404 that's where everything went down. Prada came to the door. What do I owe you the pleasure Prada stated. Prada said licking her lips J laughed in her face. Lil J was a pussy chaser he had different chicks from College chicks, Hood chicks, and the local rock head chicks. Lil J would fuck anyone and I mean anyone. Lil J walked straight in and set at the table that was been held up by crates. Listen I need to know about Candy. She fucks with that nigga Ray. Ray drives a black Hummer with 26 inch rims. Prada said on yes I know Ray with a devilish grin. Lil J just shook his head. Prada said from what I hear Ray beat the shit out of Candy. She has been in the hospital for the last 3 months. And Ray isn't leaving her side at all. My resources tells me that Candy has flat line about 2 times. And we both know my resources are on point. The

Doctors brought Candy back to life. You know Ray is a major kilo player Prada was telling Lil J, Candy has nothing but the best Doctors from what I hear.   Lil J, set there with his mouth wide open with those big ass sexy lips. Lil J, gave Prada the stepped on cocaine. Prada eyes grow wide like saucers. Thanks Lil J, Prada said. No thank you baby girl be easy now. Lil J, stood up and left ready to hit Chris up with the info. Lil J, walked back to his Audi Q7 jumped in and pulled off. Lil J. rode in silence for about 2 minutes thinking he would do anything for Chris. They have been the best of friends for over 25 years. They were so close one would think they were brothers. Lil J, Was 34 years old. Lil J, shook the thought and turned his music up. Pressing the gas on the highway. Going 85 mph listening to you Yo Gotti Pure Cocaine. Lil J. Arrived at the spot in less than 45 minutes.

Chapter 23: Chris and Lil J.

Lil J jumped out of his truck ready to tell Chris what he found out. Chris was listening to Life Jennings Must Be nice. Chris enjoyed relaxing listening to slow music. He seen his bro Lil J. walk in and cut the music down. Tiffany was Chris main chick and she was gone shopping in South Miami. So they both knew that Tiffany wouldn't be back anytime soon. Lil J. Said you're not going to believe this. Ray is moving a lot of kilos per month. Almost 2,000 kilos per month. Ray isn't just a major dope boy he is a King Pin. Ray jumped on the chick Candy. She has been in the hospital for the last 3 months. Lil J. said I don't know what the broad did. Ray beat her bad and he never left her bed side the whole 3 months she has been in the hospital. Ok bro thanks for the info Lil J. walked out leaving Chris in his thoughts. Chris set on the end of the bed and tears just begin to fall down his face. Chris had a soft spot in his heart for Candy. The crazy thing is he had only seen Candy about 5 times since he first laid eyes on her so long ago. Chris had love for Candy and he never felt like that. Not even for Tiffany and Tiffany was his main chick. Chris turned the music back up and thoughts of Candy filled his mind. Tiffany was gone she had took Chris car and went shopping in Miami. Her and one of her chicken head friends. A bitch that Chris didn't care about. Tiffany thought she was doing something when Chris gave her $3,000 dollars to go shopping. Little did she know Chris was sending her out so he could think of Candy. Chris was relaxing as the music took over his mind "Having someone who sticks around when the rough times get thick" Someone who smile is bright enough to make the projects feel like a mansion "It must be nice"

Life Jennings lyrics were so sweet to Chris ears. He knew that Candy was someone special and he had to have her By Any Means. Regardless of everything that she has been through. Chris wanted Candy to his self. Tiffany crossed his mind that gold digging bitch has to go. Chris knew the way he was living wasn't going to last. I'm going to be dead or somewhere in a Federal Penitentiary doing a life sentence. I'm going to need someone that is going to be by my side. Chris already knew Tiffany type even though she was somewhat loyal. Chris knew once the dope life ended she would hop on the next nigga dick she thought was rich. Chris had her spoiled showered her with nothing but the best gifts. Whatever name brand you can think of Tiffany had. From watches, shoes, purses you get the point whatever all the way down to the most expensive hair. Chris had the type of weave she wanted in her hair special ordered. No one in the City would have the same hair as Tiffany had in her head. Tiffany didn't really like her friends. She just used them to make herself look better. The ending of the song "Having someone to grow old with until God calls them home "Must Be Nice"

Chris could see him and Candy living together. With a family was it possible?

Chapter 24: Ray and Candy

Dr. Wan was waiting on Ray to leave the hospital. He finally left for about 3 hours to go home and cook up some dope. Agent. Price never did come back and try to speak to Candy. Agent Price had his own agenda. Agent. Price knew that he would one day meet Ray and Candy again. Agent. Price would just have to wait until that comes. Dr. Wan, walked in soon as Ray left. Candy could talk even though she was missing a couple of teeth.

Dr. Wan: Hi Candy

Candy: Hi Doc stated Candy. I wanted to thank you for everything you have done for me.

Dr.Wan: Stated I know Ray did this to you. Dr. Wan hushed Candy before she could say anything. I see this type of abuse all the time. Why won't you talk to Agent. Price?

Candy: Dr. Wan you wouldn't understand my position my life. Have you seen anyone here besides Ray? Yes of course we all know he did this to me. This is not the first time it won't be the last. This is just the worst time. In my world I trust no one. The only person I trust and love is Ray. At first I knew Ray loved me and cared for me without a doubt. Now I'm starting to think Ray hates me. Dr. Wan I can only be real with you. Through everything I have been through with Ray. I still love, care, and support and give him loyalty, trust, and understanding. And in returns I guess Ray beats me like I'm nothing as you can see for yourself. Dr. Wan I'm starting to lose my sanity. Please Dr. Wan please don't tell anyone not a soul. I want to leave Ray I just don't know how. I'm scared Ray will kill me if I try to leave. Dr. Wan just pray for me. No matter what just keep me in your prayers. Candy started to cry her hands and body started to shake.

Dr. Wan: Said Candy Cane I'll always pray for you and keep you in my heart. I'll never ever forget you. You can trust me Candy no matter what. Candy looked up and asked Dr. Wan, to leave before Ray comes back. As Dr. Wan, was walking out Candy never mention her family or friends that she once had. Candy never ever talked about her life. Or anyone she once knew.

Once Ray came back Candy was released from the hospital after 3 ½ months. Dr. Wan gave Ray orders for Candy to take it easy. As Ray wheeled Candy out of the hospital. Dr. Wan stood back and a tear fell from his eyes. As Candy looked at Dr. Wan tears fell from her eyes as well. They were connected in more ways than they both knew at the time. From that day forward Dr. Wan kept Candy in his prayers. And thought about her often throughout the day and night.

Chapter 25: Ray and Candy

Ray was waiting on Candy hand and foot. Candy eventually was able to use all her body parts again. She was finally feeling a little better she had fail into a deep depression. Candy couldn't let Ray know that she was depressed he would most likely beat her for that as well. Candy was so tired of life and how things were going. Just as she was about to get lost in her thoughts. Ray walked in their bedroom and turned off their projection screen {you know the screens like what's in the movies}. Ray sat on the end of the bed and said Candy I want you to know that I'm sorry for jumping on you like that. I lost control and I'm sorry Candy just looked at Ray. Ray starts explaining that he had lost $200,000 dollars in a dope deal gone wrong. Ray told Candy the dude that he was hooking up with. I knew his face from somewhere he just didn't know where. It's like I have seen him. Ray went to thinking I had everything lined up. The 10 kilos and the $200,000 dollars. I went to the Warehouse we were going to meet there at 8pm to do the exchange. He never showed. Ray didn't know that the person he had been doing business with was Agent. Price Ray would soon find out. Would he become a snitch? Candy was just lost in her world. She didn't want to deal with anything at this time. Ray told Candy you have an appointment tomorrow to get your teeth fixed. I can't have my sweetie walking around looking like that Ray told Candy. With that said Ray pulled out some keys and left them on the bed. Ray said come on get up let's go outside. Candy was going to protest and Ray shut up with a kiss on her lips. They both got up and walked through the French doors leading outside. Candy stood face to face with a custom made candy apple red ML63 AMG {Mercedes Benz 2015}. Candy was so excited she forgot about everything that had happen to her. She jumped on Ray and gave him the biggest hug and kiss. Ray handed her the title to the truck which was in her name Candy Cane. Candy was thinking if things ever went wrong at least she would have her two Mercedes Benz Trucks. Candy was the only one in the State that had a Candy Apple Red {ML63 AMG Mercedes Benz 2015 Truck}. Ray had paid 192,000 cash for Candy's truck. Being that the year was only 2012. Candy wanted to forget and forgive. The truck was a nice gift and she owned it. However we all know that nothing in the world is free. And everything comes with a price. One would think Candy had already paid enough.

However...

Chapter 26: Chris and Lil J.

Chris fell asleep as the ending of Must Be Nice By: Life Jennings finish playing. Tiffany had made it back from shopping why Chris was sleep. When Chris woke up Tiffany could see that something was on Chris mind. Tiffany thought to herself maybe it could be this new coke connect he met. Was the new dude not coming through with Chris kilos? Could it be he is cheating on me Tiffany thought? Tiffany would watch Chris every night as he slept. Their sex life was nothing. Their sex was once great. Tiffany use to have no limits when it came to Chris. Chris wanted more than what Tiffany was offering. Chris wanted Candy a family something that Tiffany would never be able to give him. Tiffany was raped and mutilated when she was a child. That left her unable to have children. That was something that Tiffany was insecure about. Tiffany never ever showed her insecurities and never told a lot of people that she couldn't have children. Tiffany always felt that we all hide some dark secret. That we didn't want anyone in the world to find out about. Tiffany would run kilos for Chris, Collect money and even pull the trigger on any nigga or chick that cross Chris. Tiffany was a Bonnie type of chick Chris just felt like something wasn't real about Tiffany. He could never figure it out what it was about Tiffany. Lil J had seen the change in Chris as well. Lil J wanted to know more about Candy. Lil J knew that Candy was heavy on Chris mind. Lil J wanted to find out more about Candy on his own time. And he would not be reporting to Chris. Could Lil J cross the line of loyalty to his best friend of 25 plus years? Lil J thought to his self what Chris don't know won't hurt him. Lil J was envious of Chris. The money Chris had, the contacts for cocaine, the different hoes Chris could choose from. Lil J had the same flock of chicks to choose from as well. Chris put Lil J on with dope, money and whatever else. Chris never ever thought of Lil J as a nigga that would cross him. Chris would soon find out the saying is true everything a person do in the dark comes to light.

Chapter 27: Candy

Ray had finally left Candy home alone. After he gave her
the keys and the title to her new Mercedes Benz Truck.
Candy was feeling a little excited tomorrow she would go
and get her teeth fixed. In the meantime Candy called
Chris. Candy had been thinking about Chris. He crossed her
mind a lot and she just wanted to hear Chris voice. Chris
was dark skinned on the thick side. Not fat just right with
a mouth full of diamonds. Standing at 6'0 Chris was so
handsome to Candy. A lot different than what Ray was. They
were both get money dudes. Candy knew that Chris was not
lacking in the money department. Candy wanted to be with
Chris the only problem was Tiffany. With that thought she
picked up the phone dialing Chris number (134) 666-6666 the
phone begin to ring.

Ring Ring Ring:

Chris: Yea who this

Candy: Hi Chris how are you?

Chris: Listen whoever this I don't feel like playing with
you. So don't call my phone anymore.

Candy: Wait Chris this is Candy.

Chris: Hi how are you? I been thinking a lot about you
lately. I heard about everything that happen with you.
That's a real pussy nigga you have your team. Come be with
a real nigga.

Candy: Listen Chris don't call Ray out of his name. I
didn't call to talk about him. I'm doing better to answer
your question. I have been thinking about you Chris. I need
to see you, I want to be with you. Candy last sentence was
do what you have to do. Come and save me. Before Chris
could say anything Candy hung up the phone.

Chris just stood there in one spot. Thinking Candy needs me
and wants me and I'm feeling the same way towards her. I'm
going to do whatever I have to do to make her minds. Chris
was never the one to cross anyone. As we know desperate

times calls from desperate measures. Chris would spend many minutes, hours and days plotting. Chris wanted to feel complete once and for all. Chris had money and everything he just need Candy on his side so he could wife her. Chris knew from watching and hearing that loyalty was in Candy. She was just loyal to the wrong nigga Ray. Thoughts of Chris attacked Candy. In due time we will be together Candy thought. In the meantime I will have to care and love Chris from a distance. If Ray even thought that Candy was thinking of another nigga let alone calling one. Ray would empty the clip in Candy's head without a second thought.

Chapter 28: Ray & Candy

The next morning Ray drove Candy to the dentist in her new Truck. Candy just laid her head back on the head rest. Once they arrived at the dentist and 3 hours later. Candy not only had a couple new teeth but a whole new set of lumineers. Money was never an issue when it came to Ray. Especially when he knew he had done something wrong. They left the Dentist Ray paid the Dentist $10,000 cash for Candy's new teeth. Candy could barely talk let alone open her mouth. On the way back home Candy thanked Ray for everything. Shortly after they pulled back up to their brick two story mansion. Ray said I have something nice planned for you. I know you can't open your mouth so you owe me one. Candy just laughed a little at that moment she forgot about the wrong that Ray had done. Ray carried Candy through the French doors up the stairs into their bedroom. Laid her down undressed her and started giving her oral sex. Candy and Ray's sex was always very good. Even though Ray's dick was extra little. Candy made it work she loved Ray so much. It really didn't matter to her that he was not packing in the meat department. It didn't matter if they were making love, fucking, or sucking and licking each other to death. They both fell in love all over again. Well at least one of them fell in love again. Today would be another day Ray showed Candy why he made her his main chick.

Besides Candy's loyalty and love Ray knew without a doubt he had a real life Bonnie on his team. And Ray would never ever let her go for anyone? Or would he? Ray was licking all over Candy. Saying he was going to mark his territory. Didn't Ray already owned Candy? Wasn't Candy already marching to his beat? I mean really what more could Ray want from Candy? Ray looked up and said it's either life or death you have two options. Candy was shocked she was feeling the same way once upon time about Ray. Now she was feeling like she would prefer death as long as he let her go. Candy wanted Chris and that is all she really thought about. How life would be with Chris. Candy felt Ray getting

harder with the thoughts he was having. Ray was whispering
to her life or death as he was fucking her harder and
harder. Dry fucking her at this point. A tear rolled down
her cheek and it was that moment that love ended and hate
begin. However Candy was a role player and she would get an
Oscar for the roles she was about to play with everyone
involved.

Chapter 29: Candy & Chris

Things were looking up for Ray and Candy. Candy was role playing faking like she was loving Ray. Chris found out where Candy and Ray lived. Chris was stalking and watching Ray's every move. One morning Chris watched as Ray left the house. Chris got out the car and walked up to the door. Chris twisted the knob and the door came open. The Neighborhood they lived in there was no need to lock the doors. No crimes ever happen where they were located. Houses starting out at $600,000 dollars nothing less. Chris walked up the stairs and seen Candy sleeping. He got in the bed with Candy and whispered to her. You told me to come and find you. I'm here I came for you Candy. Candy thought she was dreaming. Chris started kissing Candy at that moment she knew that she was not dreaming. Candy jumped up what are you doing here Chris. OMG you came for me? I have been thinking about you so much lately. They started French kissing each other. Candy was feeling herself getting wet and wetter. It was like her pussy was running water. Candy never ever thought about cheating on Ray. Today things would change all bets were off. Candy grab Chris 9 ½ inches and she could feel her mouth getting wet at the thought of sucking Chris dick. Letting Chris dick go without using her hands. She sucked and slurped up and down at a slow pace. Her mouth getting wetter and wetter each time her head went up and down. Candy knew that Chris was about to get stuck. One thing about Candy was she mastered the sucking dick game she was a pro at sucking dick. Candy had the best head in American. Candy not only licked his balls but his ass as well. There was no limits when it came to wanting and getting anyone. Candy had to have Chris By Any Means. Candy took Chris to another level. Chris didn't drink or smoke all he knew was Candy was drinking his babies and had some smoking ass head. OMG Candy what are you doing? Candy still sucking said well you came for me right? You came to my home the home I share with Ray. So you wanted me? Candy kept sucking until Chris got back hard. Candy got up and throw Chris down on her and Ray's bed. Not even caring that she was about to ride another nigga where Ray lay his head. Candy crawled up slowly kissing Chris from his toes all the way to his face. Got on top of Chris and rode him like she was a jockey riding a horse. Chris grab Candy's tits really hard and that made Candy even wetter. Candy and Chris never did say anything about a condom. Before you knew it Chris exploded in Candy's pussy. They both laid there holding one another sweating. Candy whispered to Chris you have to leave. You can't come back here Chris. Ray will kill me. Candy told Chris I enjoyed your sex I really want to be with you. The time is not right the time may not ever be right. I will be thinking of you. I will call you when I get a chance.

Chris please look at me and tell me that you won't come back here. Chris looked up and said Candy I will not come back here until you call for me. With that said Chris got up got dressed and walked out the house. And went straight to his car never realizing that someone was watching him the whole time. Someone was sitting in the bushes with a video recorder recording everything. Who was that someone? Chris turned the key and pulled off as thoughts of Candy filled his mind and heart. Chris rode in silence all the way back to his house.

Meanwhile back at the Federal Building Agent. Price was building a case against Ray. Agent. Price only had so far the recorded phone calls between him and Ray, Ray walking into the Warehouse with the kilos and the money. That was all Agent. Price had at this time. I need more Agent. Price said out loud.

Chapter 30: Candy

After Chris left Candy went to thinking what have I done? Ray is going to kill me if he ever finds out that Chris was in his house. Let alone that I had sex with Chris. Candy just smiled a little and the thought of Chris made her pussy wet all over again. She went and jumped in the shower. Today I'm going to go shopping. I feel like going shopping Candy was singing as she took a shower. Candy dried off and slipped into a Michael Kavilli Dress with the Matching 5 inch Michael Kavilli heels on. Throw her things in a red Michael Kavilli purse and headed out. Candy jumped into her new Benz Truck turned the music up and pulled out of her and Ray's drive way. Not realizing that a white car with dark tint was following her. Candy arrived at The Event mall about 30 minutes later. Candy was thinking about going into the new Saks Fifth Ave and Chanel store that was having a Grand Opening. Besides online shopping Candy enjoyed getting out the house sometimes to go to The Event Mall. As she was walking in she seen a pay phone. Thinking to herself I'm going to call Chris. Candy picked up the phone dialing Chris number she could feel someone watching her. When she looked around no one was there. That's strange Candy thought to herself.

Ring, Ring, Ring,

Chris: Yea who this

Candy: Your future Wife.

Chris: Hi I was just thinking about you.

Candy: I'm feeling the same way about you. My pussy is getting wet. Damn you have some awesome sex. And I would like to see you again. I need you to handle Tiffany.

Chris: What? What? How did you know about Tiffany?

Candy: Chris I know more than you think I know. I'm at The Event Mall right now. I'm thinking about swinging through to see you. I want to run a couple of things by you. I'm on a pay phone don't call my cell phone. Laughing oh I forgot you don't even have the number. I'll call you before I leave the mall. With that said candy hung up.

Chris was thinking how did Candy know about Tiffany?

Candy started shopping spending $5,000 dollars of Ray's money. She brought Chris a watch and Ray a matching watch. The only thing about Chris watch was Candy had a camera installed in it. Candy was going to record Chris every move from his voice all the way down to whoever he was sexing. Candy already had a plan in motion. One no one would ever see coming. That's if Candy don't get killed first.

Candy was thinking after getting the 2 gifts for the dudes she was having sex with. She wanted to get high Ray had kilos of cocaine in the house. There was no way that Candy could get into that cocaine. Even if she wanted to Ray had that cocaine weighed up and ready to be shipped out. Last time and that was a long time ago Candy got some cocaine it was from Chris. She had sent the BITCH Tasha to the door. That's when Candy found out Tasha was messing with Ray. Candy left out the mall and jumped in her Benz Truck taking a risk she was going to see Chris. Awwwww man Candy went to talking out loud. I forgot to call Chris and let him know I'm on my way to see him. With that thought Candy pulled over to The Book Gas Station located a pay phone. Jumped out dialing Chris #. Candy got that same feeling that someone was watching her. The only thing was that when she looked around once again there was no one there. What the fuck is going on Candy thought? Am I getting paranoid? My gut feeling tells me someone is watching me.

Ring, Ring, Ring,

Chris: Yea who this

Candy: I'm on my way click

Candy hung up

Chris went to thinking she is a trip. With that said Chris sat down on the bed and waited on Candy to arrive.

Chapter 31: Candy and Chris

Candy arrived to Chris house. Pulling up all eyes were on her. Chris seen Candy pull up in her Candy Apple Red Benz Truck he went out to meet her at the truck and walk her in the house. Candy hug Chris and gave him a kiss on the lips. It's good to see you again Chris. You know I want some cocaine Chris. Chris was like yea I know that. That was the thing about Chris. Candy could always be open and honest with him about anything. No matter what it was and Chris never ever looked down on her. Candy once felt like that about Ray. But over a period of time things had changed between Candy and Ray. Candy was seeking to destroy Ray or get destroyed. It is a dog eat dog world. And Candy wasn't going to get eaten alive. With those thoughts and Chris still kissing all over Candy. Chris stopped kissing on Candy. And said come on let's get you some cocaine. Chris went under his king size bed and pulled out a whole brick of cocaine. Candy's pussy got so wet from seeing the cocaine. Candy knew it was going to be some good coke. It was straight off the kilo no cut in it whatsoever. Chris just cut Candy off a whole corner without even weighting it or anything. Candy took the cocaine and put it in her purse. Candy told Chris listen I have a plan and I need you to help me out on this. It's either your with me or not. Chris looked Candy in the eyes and said I'm with you. I want you to become my wife. Your my future your too good of a person to be with a fuck nigga like Ray. Candy said listen Chris what did I tell you about calling him out of his name. Aren't you with Tiffany? Isn't that your ride or die chick? Chris said listen Candy I don't want her I'm serious I love you Candy. With that said Candy already knew that she had Chris in her pocket. Just where she wanted him. Chris didn't realize that Candy was a role player Candy was a gamer. She played a lot of mind games with a lot of different people. Would her games backfire on her? What was going to happen? What does Candy really want from Chris? Candy looked Chris in the eyes without a smile or a care in the world. Chris if you love me like you say you do. Show me show me that you love me and want to be with me and only me. With that said Candy walked up to Chris licking softly in his ear. Get rid of Tiffany by Any Means. I don't care what you have to do you get rid of her. I'm your future wife right Chris? Chris spoke softly yes Candy you are. Slipping his fingers in Candy pussy flicking her spur tongue. Candy came fast with the thought of Chris fingering fucking her and the cocaine. It was just a matter of minutes before she came all over Chris fingers. Candy said take them out and suck on them. Taste me Chris without a second thought Chris did just that. Talk about mind control at its best. Candy backed away from Chris grab her purse. And gave Chris the watch with the camera in it that she had purchased. I brought this for you do you like it? Yes Chris answered I do like it a lot. Thank you Candy. Candy said Chris I mean what I said. Chris said don't worry future wife I got you. It's done walking out of Chris room and into the living room. That is when Candy eyes met Lil J's eyes. Candy thinking oh my fucking GOD who is he? Chris, was walking behind Candy. She was so lost in her thoughts she didn't even know that Chris was behind her. Candy this is my best friend, Homeboy something like a brother Lil J. Hi Lil J nice to meet you. My name is Candy Cane. With that said Candy and Chris walked out the house. Once again Candy felt that feeling that someone was watching her. Chris do you feel like someone was watching us? Chris looked around no I don't see anyone. Oh ok thinking nothing more of it Candy jumped in her truck and waved good-bye at Chris.

Who was the person that had been watching Candy? Hiding in the bushes? Following Candy around the City. Who was this Mysterious person?

Chapter 32: Candy

Candy pulled off thinking to herself so much be happening. And it's happening fast with Chris and I. Candy went to thinking about the cocaine that Chris had given to her. Candy pulled over on side of the road and got out and paid the meter. Set in her truck and got higher than a kite. Damn this is some good cocaine Candy thought to herself. Candy set in her truck getting high by herself. With thoughts of Chris and Ray. Candy kept snorting the coke and the thoughts consumed her easily. She thought more of Chris and less of Ray. The plan was for Chris to destroy himself with a little help from Candy. Candy already did what she needed to do and that was give Chris the watch with the camera in it. And Ray would do the rest. Candy could feel the cocaine draining in her mouth. This is the time that Candy could give the best head. When her mouth was numb. Candy would suck on Ray's dick for 3 hours straight why playing in her pussy. She would pay dearly the next day when her mouth was sore and she could barely open it. That's how Ray knew that Candy was high. Ray was trying to figure out who was giving Candy cocaine. Ray just could never put his finger on the person. Ray had always wanted Candy to stop snorting cocaine. Ray knew what cocaine could do to someone who couldn't control their habit. Ray had seen the cocaine downfall one, two, many times. Candy set there in that same spot for the next 2 hours. Just snorting her cocaine crying, thinking, laughing and listening to music in her truck. That was something that Candy enjoyed doing. Just chilling, relaxing and getting high by herself.

Chapter 33: Candy and Ray

Ray had been calling Candy for the past 2 hours. Ray had been pacing the floor of their home. Worried, mad and pissed off as hell. He couldn't reach Candy. Ray picked up his phone again and dialed Candy's #

Ring, Ring, Ring

Candy: Hello

Ray: Where the fuck are you? I been calling your motherfucking phone for 2 hours straight.

Candy: I went to The Event Mall, I went and got my nails and toes done, I went by the rim shop on 145th Street. I went to get some rims for my new truck. I'm on my way home now.

Ray: Ok I'm waiting on you I love you Candy.

Candy: Hung up without saying she loves Ray.

Candy was always quick with the lies. Especially when it came down to Ray. There was no way she could tell Ray the TRUTH!!!! Candy stopped getting high stuck her straw and the rest of her cocaine in her pussy. Candy went to thinking gosh I need to go home Ray is waiting on me. But I'm running low on cocaine. What am I going to do? Candy knew for a fact that she didn't waste any coke. Candy couldn't believe that she had set there and snorted almost the whole bag of cocaine. Candy wanted to go back to Chris. She couldn't that would make her about 2 more hours away from home. Ray would really trip on her.

DAMN!!!!! DAMN!!!!!! DAMN!!!!!!

Candy was pissed off. She started her truck and drove home high as hell, horny and wanting to suck some dick, eat some ass and get fucked however and where ever. DAMN!!!!! Candy said out loud talking to herself. I hope this nigga Ray don't be with the bullshit when I get home. Candy stopped by The City Sex Store which was the biggest Sex Store in Press More. Jumped out her Benz truck ran in purchased some new lingerie and some new sex toys. She was back on the road in less than 10 minutes. All the other toys her and Ray had been used. And she wanted to try something new. That's if Ray wasn't tripping. Once Candy got in the house she dropped her bags. Went and jumped in the shower without speaking to Ray. Candy always took a shower before and after sex. That was just something that Candy always did. She wanted to take the last hit of the cocaine. Also before Ray went to playing in her pussy. That was just something that Ray always did when Candy came back home. Ray had it bad he would check her, smell her panties, make her open her legs. He would check her butt hole, and everything. Ray was anything but normal. Candy got out of the shower about 10 minutes later. High and ready she walked into the room with a green lingerie on that was Ray's favorite color.

Hi baby Candy said.

How are you today? Ray asked giving her a kiss.

You like this new lingerie set I have on Ray? Yes I do it's very nice. I brought you something new from The Event Mall Ray. Let me see go and get it with that said Candy went and got the watch out of the bag and gave it to Ray. She explained to Ray that it was waterproof and he could keep it on at all times. He liked the watch very much and said thank you. Ray mentioned that he was upset at Candy. And he asked her why were you missing for 2 hours straight? Candy didn't say anything she couldn't think fast enough. Between been high and wanting to fuck Candy couldn't think of anything to say. So she said NOTHING!! Instead she took Ray's dick and started sucking it. Ray was moaning just when Candy was really getting into sucking his dick real good. Ray pulled her up. Ray yelled BITCH I know your back getting high. You most likely never stopped getting high. Let me find out Candy for a fact that you're cheating on me. I'm going to kill you and I am not playing with you. Mark my words Candy I WILL KILL YOU!!!!!!!!!!!! Candy couldn't say anything she already knew what Ray was capable of doing. Candy didn't really have any worries. She was going to have to take Ray out before he took her out. By Any Means!!!!!!!!!!!!!!

Candy got up from between Ray's legs. And yelled at him all this shit you putting me through since I met you. GOT DAMN RIGHT I AM HIGH!!!!!!!! SO FUCKING WHAT!!!!!!!!!!!!!! I want to fuck Ray is that ok with you? Do I need your permission to fuck you? Yes or fucking no? Candy yelled at Ray. Or would you prefer me go fuck and suck someone else? Would you like that Ray? Why did Candy say that? Ray walked up to Candy and grab her mouth. What the fuck did you say to me you fucking BITCH? Candy said WOULD YOU LIKED ME TO FUCK AND SUCK ON SOMEONE ELSE? Ray punched her and kicked her Candy just laid there and laughed. Yea Ray I'm used to your bullshit it doesn't even matter to me anymore. I enjoyed myself before I came home. So you can go ahead and kick my ass. Just know Ray I'm not going to always be here for you to kick my ass. One day I'm going to walk away from you and leave you high and fucking dry. You hear me Ray? High and fucking dry now you think you kicking my ass, pulling my hair, breaking bones, punching out teeth you think that is going to what Ray? Make me love you more? What are you trying to install in me Ray fear? Well Ray since your always beating me guess what you have installed in me. HATE!!!!!!!!!!!!!! Now Ray kick this ass and I'm going to still suck your little ass dick and fuck you. Like I said that is what I want to do. Candy just laughed and laughed after about 45 minutes and another bloody mouth. Candy got up off the floor and did just what she wanted to do from the start. And that is suck and fuck Ray. Candy fucked him and sucked him so good he came in 2 minutes flat. That's how Ray was Candy believe that Ray felt in control when he beat on her. Little did Ray know he had already lost all control. Over the many years of abuse, different girls, the nice gifts after she got beat on over and over time and time again. Candy stop caring and that is when she started role playing. Ray fail fast off to sleep. Candy got up and once again she was back in the mirror looking ugly with scars on every part of her body. Candy set on the toilet thinking Ray has to go I can't keep going through this. I just can't with those thoughts Chris popped up in her mind. She went to thinking what was Chris up to? What was he doing at that very moment? Would he treat Candy like Ray? Candy already knew that Chris sex was so much better than Ray. With those thoughts Candy found herself playing in her pussy. Thinking of Chris with his thick tall handsome self. Than her thoughts with to his friend Lil J damn he was handsome as well with those lips and he had a small gap in his teeth he was still sexy as hell.

DAMN!!!!!!!!!!!!!! Just as thoughts of Lil J attacked her mind she came all over her fingers. And it felt so damn good. Candy had forgot about the scars, the headache, the backache, and the sore bones for 5 minutes. DAMN!!!!!!!!!! DAMN!!!!!!!!! DAMN!!!!!!!!!! I have to get myself together. Candy went downstairs to try to get some ice she already knew that she had to play doctor on herself. Candy didn't realize that Ray had many treats up his sleeve as well. Ray has installed cameras in the bathrooms in their home. Candy thought she was the only one that was slick and could play the game. Ray was old School he knew all the tricks. Just like most niggas in the world they will all fall victim to some smoking ass head, a pretty face, and wet good pussy with no smell. Candy would later find out a lot of things about Ray. How far he was really willing to go? What will Candy do? Will Ray eventually cross Candy? What's going to happen?

Chapter 34: Agent Price & Dr. Wan

Agent Price never stopped thinking about the girl in the Hospital. Dr. Wan decided to reach out to Agent Price. Dr. Wan was also concerned about Candy. He prayed for her every night.

Ring, Ring, Ring

Federal Agent Price speaking

Agent Price, this is Dr. Wan calling. Have you heard anything from Candy yet? Have you found out anything on Ray?

Federal Agent Price, Of course I'm in the process of building a Federal Case against Rayshawn. As known as Ray. I can't get into details over the phone. I'll be in contact with you as soon as possible.

Federal Agent Price told Dr. Wan ok Dr. Wan said and hung up the phone.

Federal Agent Price and Dr. Wan mission was to save Candy from Ray. Or will they end up hurting Candy more trying to save her?

Chapter 35: Chris And Lil J

Chris was excited to see that Lil J had made it back home. Lil J had a made a dope run to New York City. Chris and Lil J was not dealing with rookies in the dope game they were major players. Lil J asked Chris about Candy. Brother, she looks damn good when I saw her the other week coming out your room. She is beautiful Chris and I'm not even lying. Chris stated Lil J her heart is just as beautiful. I want her to myself I have to have her bro. And her pussy taste so good Chris told Lil J. Lil J just set there with his own agenda thinking in his head. I want to taste what you tasted. However, he could never ever let Chris know that he was really a HATER. That was one thing about Lil J he was just a dude that rode alone getting money on the side. He never had his own limelight he was under Chris. Of course just like most niggas they want to outshine even the person that is helping them and want to see them make it in the dope game. Chris always put Lil J on gave him dope, money, and they fucked chicks together. Lil J knew that Chris was loving Candy Chris always stressed to Lil J that Candy would be his future wife. Lil J told Chris I hear you. Chris was stressing it is something different about her. Lil J had never seen Chris so head over heels over anyone before. Lil J had his own agenda Lil J was willing to show Chris this BITCH!!!!! Isn't no better than anyone else. Would Lil J succeed on his mission? Some lines you would think a person will not cross. Like they say all is fair in love and war. Isn't it?

Chapter 36: Chris and Lil J

Lil J was on his own mission to destroy Chris. Lil J HATED Chris with a passion. If you would have seen them you would have never knew how Lil J really felt about Chris. Lil J was a role player as well. Lil J played many different roles in his life. Chris would always show love to Lil J. When he got of jail Chris would give him $10,000 cash and 62 grams of pure cocaine to get on his feet with. 62 grams of cocaine was 2.186 ounces enough to send you to a Federal Prison. Chris always was a risk taker he took Federal chances all the time. Chris wasn't scared of anything. Unlike Lil J he was straight PUSSY he was afraid of his own shadow. No one ever knew why Lil J HATED Chris so much. Maybe it was something more going on that no one knew about. They were friends since they were little. Chris beat the shit out of Lil J a long time ago when they were still in diapers and Lil J held a grudge for that. Who the fuck knows. It could have been that they had information on one another that could send the other one away for a lifetime. They did do a lot of dirt together. Chris never ever knew that Lil J felt this way about him. Soon he would find out. At what cost?

Chapter 37: Federal Agent Price

Agent Price had put in a call to speak to one of his Judge friends. Agent Price had connections with Lawyers, Judges, even the Mayor everyone knew Agent Price. Agent Price had so many Awards he was maxed out on the pay scale. Making $90,000 a year as a Federal Agent. Agent Price lived for this type of work. He was 6'2 brown skinned, with 4 open face gold's, 35 years old, with no kids, single and drove a black on black 2013 Charger. Agent Price had a low fade and if a person wasn't too careful they would think he was a dope dealer. Agent Price had just received on his desk the warrant to tap Rayshawn's phones house phone, and cell phone. Agent Price already knew that Ray was a kingpin in the dope game and moved major kilos from State to State. Agent. Price knew that Ray was a major kingpin after not meeting him at the Warehouse. Instead Agent. Price was laying low taking a million pictures of Ray. Without Ray even knowing. That was the good thing about been a Federal Agent. No one really knew anything about Agent. Price and is for some reason they did find out that Agent. Price was a Federal Agent he couldn't be touched. No one knew that Agent Price and Ray were from the same side of town. Over by the Dog Tracks. They just took different paths in life. Ray made Agent Price yearly salary in 2 weeks. Agent Price wanted Ray behind bars. By Any Means and he would not stop until he arrested Ray himself. Agent Price called up "Best "and the tap was placed on the Ray's phone service.

Chapter 38: Candy And Ray

After having sex with Ray they had both fallen asleep. Candy always put in more work than Ray. She was just find with that Candy was more aggressive than Ray. Ray phone had woke them both up.

Ray: Yo

An unknown voice: I need those as soon as possible.

Ray: Cool I'm on my way to the Warehouse.

Ray got up and brushed his teeth got dressed kissed candy. Grabbed his black duffle bag and left. The duffle bag was full of kilos of coke. Ray left out the house and jumped in his car not knowing that Agent. Price was doing surveillance on him. Agent Price was taking pics of Ray. Listening to all of his phone calls. All the while trailing behind him. Building a case that would change not only Ray life but Candy, Chris, Tiffany, Parda and Lil J as well.

Chapter 39: Ray and Prada

Ray had dropped off the duffle bag and picked up $150,000 cash. Ray wanted some quick head and pussy even though it was 4:15am. Candy was at home sleeping that didn't even matter to Ray. Ray called Prada his jump off chick.

Ring, Ring, Ring,

Prada: Hi baby I've been waiting on you to come see me.

Ray: BITCH!!!!! Shut up I'm on my way take your nasty whore as a bath. I know you been fucking. I got something for your bitch ass anyways.

Prada: Said ok and hung

Ray just laughed dumb ass bitch do anything for some cocaine. Even though Ray fought Candy and acted like he didn't give a damn half of the time. Ray knew he was wrong for stepping out on Candy. Ray just thought he could do whatever to Candy whenever to Candy and she would still stick around through it all. Little did Ray know Candy was doing her own dirt. Eventually Ray pulled up to The Pork and Pork Projects. Ray already know that Prada was on cocaine very bad and that was what she wanted. Prada was waiting on Ray soon as he got in she got her knees and started sucking his little ass dick making noise like his dick was a microphone and she was speaking into it.

Ray didn't even have to tell her what to do she already knew her position. That was down on her knees. Ray would never kiss Prada he knew that Prada sucked dicked for cocaine, ate pussy for cocaine and whatever else for cocaine. Prada knew she wasn't anything to Ray. She had accepted her faith long time ago when it came down to dealing with Ray. Prada knew that Ray and Candy were together. That just made Prada go harder for Ray. She was willing to do anything to get Ray and I mean anything. Just as Ray was about to cum he grab Prada nappy hair. Prada didn't even have money for weave her hair was just short and very nappy. Ray didn't even care that Prada was chocking and tears forming in her eyes. He just kept mouth fucking her and hitting the back of her mouth with his dick. Harder and harder and harder over and over again. Isn't that how you do BITCHES AND HOES? Ray thought to himself? He throw on the floor 1 gram of cut cocaine. And he watched as she crawled around on her knees looking for the coke. Ray thought to himself that BITCH is gone off that SHIT dumb ass whore. As Ray walked out the Apartment to his car. Not knowing that Agent Price was watching taking pictures and timed how long Ray was in Prada Apartment.

Agent. Price said out loud while taking the last picture. Soon Ray very soon your time is limited you just don't know.

Chapter 40: Chris, Tiffany And Lil J.

Chris was wondering when he would see Candy again. Chris had put Tiffany in her own little place. Nothing fancy in the GHETTO. Just a little something that would keep Tiffany away from him. Tiffany was getting on Chris last nerves. Chris wanted to get rid of Tiffany just as he had promised Candy. How? Chris went to thinking. Tiffany knew a lot about Chris whole operation. Would Tiffany tell everything she knew? If she felt Chris wanted someone other than her? Lil J and Tiffany were in bed together. Tiffany had just finished riding Lil J's dick. Chris didn't know they were having sex behind his back. Tiffany leaned over and kissed Lil J in his mouth. Lil J told her Chris has to go. I know Chris isn't feeling me anymore Lil J told Tiffany. Lil J said well Tiffany to be honest with you Chris is head over heels in love with Candy. Candy!!!!! Candy!!!!! Tiffany jumped up yelling. Tiffany tits and everything were flying everywhere. Tiffany was a good 5'11. Tiffany looked like she was 35. Tiffany was only 26 years old. Tiffany had a hard life growing up. Tiffany struck rose gold when she met Chris. Tiffany couldn't have children and of course Chris dreamed of a family. Tiffany knew that Chris had put Tiffany out of the main house for a reason. She just didn't know what the reason was. Now she knows that Chris is caring and loving someone else. Tiffany had heard that Candy was messing a kingpin name Rayshawn better known as Ray. And that Ray and Candy lived in the City in a 2 story brick mansion. She wondered how Chris knew Candy. With that thought Tiffany jumped back in bed with Lil J. Not only did Tiffany suck Lil J's dick but she allowed him to fuck her in the ass, and she ate his ass, Lil J ate her pussy and they fell off to sleep with ass, and cum on their breath.

Chapter 41: Chris

Chris had been calling Lil J for 2 days straight with no answer. Chris was thinking where was his runner? The thought never crossed his mind that his best friend was laying up with Tiffany. All the dope was in the house with Chris. So he knew that Lil J wasn't locked up somewhere. Lil J must have been with one of his whore's. One day soon Chris would find out which one of his whore's. Would he care that Lil J was sleeping with Tiffany? His main girlfriend? Chris never really loved anyone but his Mother. Chris was an only child he never knew his Father. Growing up Chris had a hard life. His Mother wasn't able to give Chris all the finer things in life. Chris had to wear Champion Shoes, No name brand clothes, dirty clothes that didn't fit at all. All the kids at School laughed at Chris. Chris watched his Mother get beat on by different dudes that came in and out of their life. Chris would stand in the corner and watch and the dudes use his Mother as a punching bag. Standing there alone with tears in his eyes. Chris used to feel helpless growing up and knew that his Mother always loved him and cared for him. Chris knew that for fact there was never a doubt in Chris mind. Since the first day he laid his eyes on Candy. He knew he would never ever be able to walk away from her. It was something that was Mysterious about Candy. Chris never told anyone about his life growing up. You would be fooled by the hard exterior especially once you got to know him how sweet, loving, caring, loyal and honest he really was. Don't get it twisted Chris would fight, shoot or whatever to get his point across. Chris GREED!!!!!! Had consumed him he wanted more money, more dope, more money, more dope. Chris always wanted to be the best and the biggest in whatever he did in life. All he really wanted was real honest love without the strings attached to it. Would Chris find that love in Candy?

As We Know Life Offers So Many
Twist And Turns!!!!!!!!!!!!

Chapter 42: Lil J & Chris

Lil J finally came back around like he wasn't around Tiffany. Lil J was a top of the line role player.

Chris: What's up bro where you been?

Lil J: Fucking... nigga where else?

Chris: Just laughed and said I feel you bro.

Lil J asked Chris has he heard from Candy. Chris said no he hasn't heard from her. Not since the last time he talked to her. Chris didn't know that Lil J had a hidden agenda.

Chapter 43: Chris, Lil J, Tiffany

After about an hour Chris, Lil J and Tiffany. We're relaxing in the living room. Tiffany had come over to get some money of course from Chris. Chris only gave her $400.00 to go shopping. Tiffany blew Lil J a kiss when Chris went into the other room to get the money. Lil J whispered with his big ass lips. I want to fuck you tonight. Tiffany said ok Lil J I will let my home girl know. They never knew that Chris seen the whole thing play out. Chris really never went into the room.

DAMN!!!! SNAKES ARE EVERYWHERE!!!!!!!

I have to start watching everyone this nigga been my friend for over 25 years and he does this? That was the difference between Lil J and Chris. Lil J was weak for some pussy and head. Chris was getting money and moving kilos of cocaine.

Chapter 44: Chris

Chris couldn't believe what he had just seen with his own 2 eyes. Chris had 20/20 vision he didn't need glasses so he knew what he really seen was correct. It wasn't a joke Tiffany and Lil J were fucking behind Chris back. Lil J and Tiffany had to go as soon as possible.

Chapter 45: Ray, Candy, and Agent Price

Candy had been thinking about Ray for the past 2 hours. It wasn't like Ray not to call her at least every 30 minutes. If Ray hadn't called her in about an hour. Candy was going to call every Police Station, Hospital in the City to try and find Ray.

Ring, Ring, Ring

Ray: Yea Sweetie

Candy: Hi baby I was just calling you to see what's up. Where are you?

Ray: I'm rolling you already know not to question me.

Candy: Laughed a little and said your right baby. I was just thinking about you. I love you

Ray: I love you to.

Click they both hung up.

Agent. Price you got that recorded?

He asked his co-worker? Yes I got it.

Candy wanted to tell Ray something but she knew that over the phone was not the way to tell Ray. Candy would wait on Ray to arrive home. If the Streets didn't teach Candy anything. They taught her to always watch her surroundings. Listen close and say least as possible. Even when Candy is high she is quite and just looks around. Unless she is with ray fucking and sucking on him and of course getting her ass beat. As candy got lost in her thoughts her best friend Diamond. Crossed her mind Diamond was so different than Candy. Candy was thinking about one night Ray beat he up a long time ago. He throw bricks at her kicked her all in the back. If Ray would have kept kicking her over, over and over again. Ray was going crazy that night for some strange reason. Still to this day Candy doesn't even know why Ray was so mad. If he would have kept kicking her Candy would have been paralyzed from the waist down from spinal injuries. Candy was walking down 200th Street in the City.

Trying to get to Diamonds house. Diamond stayed on 300th Street. Was Candy going to make it? Candy seen a jeep coming and stood in the middle of the road crying. The lady stop Candy said please, please, please, give me a ride. My boyfriend Ray just beat me up please. The lady was scared and skeptical but she gave Candy a ride to her best friend Diamond's house. Once Candy got there she passed out on the porch and Diamond had to call the Ambulance for Candy. Diamond was always praying and going to Church. That night Diamond was praying that her best friend of 15 plus years be ok. Candy was missing Diamond so much. Everything that was happening in life Candy didn't have anyone to share anything with. Diamond never judged Candy and Diamond knew that Candy use to get high off cocaine. Candy would go to Diamonds house and lay on her big 40E size tits and cry herself to sleep. Candy was thinking when the time is right she will pick up the phone and call Diamond. In hopes that Diamond would still be the same person she left alone for Ray over 10 years ago. Thoughts of Diamond faded fast as she heard the alarm sound. Candy knew that had to be Ray. Candy met Ray in the kitchen. Hey babe I miss you Candy said. Ray kissed her and said I miss you as well.

Candy said Ray I have something to tell you. What? Well today when you left I looked out the window. And there was a black on black charger following you. They were looking as if they were watching the house. And your point is? Ray said. Ray it just doesn't seem right something isn't right I'm trying to tell you. I was just telling you Ray that's all. Ray asked Candy have you had some cocaine today. Yes Ray I did I have some. Candy still kind of cared for Ray. Even though things were all messed up all the time. Ray had everything house, cars, money, dope, clothes, shoes, jewelry, but everything meant nothing to Candy. All Candy wanted was to be love and give love point blink period. Didn't everyone want that? Unconditional Real Love? The only thing is how far would one go to get it?

Ray didn't know if to believe Candy or not. Or just blame it on her been high off cocaine.

Ray did know that whoever was selling Candy cocaine had to be seen about by him. Ray couldn't leave Candy in her current situation or could he? Would he have no other choice? Ray said I tell you what whenever we talk on the phone. If I never ever tell you I love you. You know something is wrong. If you call me and end the call without saying you love me than I know something is wrong on your end. And I know not to come home. Don't ever forget Candy Ray said. Don't forget ever never ever forget that's our code. Ray also told Candy no matter what happens. Who says I said what, did what, said anything about you. Don't you ever fold under pressure. That's the Police, Federal Agents Jobs to scare you into saying something you don't need to say. Tell them if they ever come you need a Lawyer and never ever try and talk your way out of a situation. Ray wasn't taking any chances. Ray knew that he was a kingpin with millions and millions of Dollars, Business, Property, Boats, and Real Estate all over the United States all illegal gained from Drug Profits. Ray had off shore accounts that he didn't even let anyone Know about not even Candy or his family. Ray already knew once the Federal Agents came for him they would take everything away from him. Everything that he owned they would take it all. That's if he ever slipped into the Federal Agents hands. Ray had 1 rule since he was a little boy running dope around the City. Before he became a King Pin Never ever deal with anyone new always keep the same clientele. Little did Ray know Agent Price had him on his radar. Ray and Candy got dressed and went out to eat at a 5 Star Restaurant.

Ray didn't know that Agent. Price had already boxed Candy off in her Candy Apple Benz truck. Agent. Price had told Candy that he had enough evidence against Ray and her to hide them up under a Federal Prison for life. He told Candy you need to become an informant. Are you going to help yourself and Ray? What are you going to do? Agent. Price asked Candy. Before he could say anything Candy started to cry. Let me think about it. At that time Agent. Price told Candy I have 2 people on my target list already. Candy stopped crying and asked Agent. Price who? Agent. Price said with the straight face. Chris and Lil J.

Candy said what? Agent. Price you heard me correct Chris and Lil J. You know those two players really well don't you Candy? Candy gave Agent. Price the look of death. If her look could kill he would be dead. Agent. Price said the only rule to becoming an informant with the Federal Bureau of Investigation {FBI} you can't tell anyone. I'll get back with you soon Agent. Price told Candy. In the meantime keep role playing. With that said Agent. Price walked back to his black on black charger started his car and left. How did he know I was a role player? Damn he looks like someone I have met before Candy thought to herself.

With tears in her eyes. Candy knew what needed to be done. This is not what I signed up for. Fuck Ray how, where, and when did you slip?

Chapter 46: Ray

Ray was trying to enjoy his meal he couldn't shake the thought of going to a Federal Prison. What if he was been watch? Ray only dealt with the Mexicans. As far as cash goes he didn't owe anyone no money and he only served kilos of cocaine to his same clientele. Ray made sure Candy was good he took her on trips around the world, expensive shopping trips, Exotic Vacations. They ate at the best 5 star restaurants. Ray had given Candy everything. Was everything enough for Candy? Ray just looked at Candy sitting across from him. Candy could feel his eyes on her. Candy knew Ray so well you would have thought she was the blood that pumped through his body. Candy asked without looking up what's wrong Ray? What are you thinking about? Ray I'm not worried about anything Candy. Loyalty and Love over everything. Don't you ever forget death before dishonor Ray said to Candy.

Candy looked up and excused herself to go to the restroom. Candy went to the restroom and pulled out her cocaine. She needed to get high. Candy already knew that she had signed a deal with the DEVIL. A contract that she was not sure she could honor.

Would Candy pay with DEATH? Or dishonesty?

Chapter 47: Chris, Lil J & Tiffany

Chris was always the one person not to cross. Chris knew many killers and Chris was a killer. The only people he really loved and cared about was his mother. Chris knew that he couldn't let his guard down once his mother past away in 2010. Once he seen Candy again he felt like he could open up and love again. Tiffany was just a BITCH he knew would eventually cross him. Chris didn't won't to call his killers that were on standby. At any moment the killers were ready to put on their all black, hide in bushes and wait to carry out a hit on anyone. When I say anyone I mean anyone from babies, to children, to Grandma's, anyone could be killed if the killers were called. Chris wanted his own sweet revenge he wanted and would get Lil J and Tiffany. Chris knew that Lil J wanted money and hoes. Little did Lil J know this would be his last trip to New York City, Chris would kill 2 birds with 1 stone. Chris had pre packed 2,000 grams of cocaine in Lil J car. Lil J already knew the route as he had made this trip so many times before. Lil J thought as Chris told him I need you to take Tiffany with you. Lil J went to thinking I'm going to fuck the shit out of her, go to the beach, hang out and get money. Bro Lil J asked what's up. Why you want me to take Tiffany with me? I have something to handle and I need her out of my hair for a couple of days Chris stated. OK Lil J that's fine with me. I'll take her with me. A stamp was already on the 2,000 grams of cocaine.

Revenge Is a Mother Fucker!!!!!

Chapter 48: Chris, Lil J AND TIFFANY

Lil J and Tiffany would be trafficking 70.547 ounces of cocaine. That would equal 2 kilos of pure fish scale cocaine. Enough to get them both life plus 50 years in a Federal Prison. Chris had already made the call to Candy. Chris told her to call up Agent. Price and have all Federal Agents in 5 States to be on the lookout for a red Magnum with a paper tag. The Federal Agents loved these types of case. Where the people telling wanted nothing in return for their information. Chris just wanted Lil J and Tiffany GONE and out of the way forever. Lil J and Tiffany would have no clue that Chris had set them up. They would be traveling over 4,000 miles with 2 kilos of cocaine. Chris couldn't wait to get the call that they were both in handcuffs. The Federal Agents had already set up points and Undercover Agents at every rest stop. In between each State they would cross. To get to New York City. Lil J and Tiffany would go down in history. Everyone from Down South all the way up to the North, East and West Coast would know that Chris was not the one to cross. Chris knew from this day forward not to ever trust anyone else. Or would he let his guard down? Will he eventually pay the ultimate price seeking love?

Chapter 49: Tiffany & Lil J

Let's go Tiffany said Lil J. They had stopped for gas at the "Place Gas Station "I have to get this shipment up North. What they didn't know that Chris had cameras and a GPS Tracking Device in the car. The Federal Agents will have everything they needed to build their case and present it to a Federal Judge. When someone called in information and didn't want anything in return the Federal Agents didn't have to get a warrant for anything. In this case the Federal Agents knew for a fact that everything that told was the truth. There would be 2 kilos of cocaine in the car without a doubt. The Federal Agents were listening in on everything. They allowed Tiffany and Lil J to travel for many miles. The more miles they traveled the more charges they would get. Once they cross a State line into another State they will have on top of the many other charges Interstate Charges. The Federal Agents listened as Lil J and Tiffany laughed and carried on about how they had betrayed Chris. How much money Lil J had stolen form Chris, How Chris was in love with Candy and wanted to wife her, Lil J told Tiffany all types of stuff him and Chris were doing with different females. Tiffany was all ears and so were the Federal Agents. The Federal Agents were listening giving each other a high five as they were digging a bigger hole than they were already in. Without their knowledge wasn't there a risk in everything you do anyways? Didn't Lil J and Tiffany think about someone other than their own selfish wants?

Chapter 50: Ray and Candy

Candy was super high once she came out of the restroom. Candy couldn't even finish her food.

Are you done Ray?

Yea Candy I'm done are you ready to go?

Ray tipped the waiter $250.00. Ray always felt good about helping out people. Especially those that had to work hard for an honest living. Ray just wasn't going to get a job. Ray could never ever see working from 9am-5pm for pennies on the dollar. Ray wasn't talking much on the ride home. That was fine with Candy she was sitting back enjoying her high. Ray was in his own thoughts. Thinking he had to get legit and fast. Ray always wanted to get out the dope game. Ray was in so deep with the Mexican Cartel. It was no way the Mexicans would let Ray just walk away like that. Ray ordered up $50,000 grams 1,763.7 ounces of cocaine every week from the Mexicans. That would equal 5 kilos of cocaine. Ray never cheated or stole from the Cartel. And always had his cash up front. The kilos of cocaine were going for $40,000 each. The Mexicans gave Ray a good deal. Ray had been dealing with the Mexican Cartel since the early 90's. Money was not an issue to Ray. Ray had more than enough. Candy finally said something that broke the tension in the car. The tension was so thick you could cut it with a knife. Ray for the last time it's going to be ok Candy Said. For the first time in a long time Candy wasn't. Candy knew things would be ok for Ray. Candy only wish Ray would get out the dope game for good. Would Candy help him get out and stay out? What will Candy do? Will she fold under pressure? Is she going to turn on Ray?

Candy knew her place very well. She would never say much about Ray Career choice. Ray finally pulled up at their mansion. Drops Candy off at home. Candy said see you later Ray.

With that said Candy stood in the doorway and watched as Ray pulled off. Before he got out of the driveway good. Ray had pulled his phone out of his pocket.

Ring, Ring, Ring

Hello Prada said.

Ray: Bitch I'm on my way you know the drill.

Prada: Hangs up the phone

Chapter 51: Prada

Prada knew how much Ray was worth. She also knew that she wasn't going to be a fool for Ray much longer. Prada wanted Ray to herself to be in her life forever and with those thoughts. Prada got a pin and stuck tiny holes in the condom. The oldest trick in the book of trying to trap a nigga with a baby. Prada knew that Ray never looked at the condom when he came over. He never brought his own condoms to her house. Prada could tell that Ray was stressed out about something. She didn't know exactly what it was. Prada knew that she wanted everything that she heard that Ray was giving Candy. Prada and Ray had been fucking each other for over 9 years on the down low. Ray was still giving Prada dick and coke nothing more nothing less. In 9 years Ray never kissed Prada or anything. Prada had pulled out all the works. Once Ray called she jumped in the shower, lite some candles, and put on something sexy. It was one thing that Ray and Candy didn't have together. Tonight Prada would make sure she did whatever to stay in Ray life forever. Soon after Ray arrived at "The Pork and Pork Projects "knocked on Prada door. Prada was shocked that Ray wasn't calling her names once she opened the door. Ray followed Prada in her room. Took off his clothes and laid on the bed. Prada already knew never to kiss Ray. She wasn't getting her pussy ate by Ray or anything that would turn her on completely. Prada knew already that she had to do all the work. Treat Ray like a king and suck his dick, eat his ass, and allow him to fuck hers. Prada knew that the condom had holes in it that is something that Ray didn't know. All she had to do was suck on Ray's little ass dick. Slip the condom on and ride him backwards. He would nut Prada would suck his dick again with the condom still on and his dick would get hard again. Then she would let Ray fuck her in the ass with the dry condom on and he would nut again in her ass. The nut would come leak through the condom little by little. Prada did this about 6 times until she could no longer suck his dick anymore. Prada allowed Ray to nut in the condom which really had holes in it every time. Ray was like most dudes that he didn't give a damn BITCH, HOE, WIFEY as long as she had some smoking ass head.

Prada was A1 and that was Ray's weakness for Prada. After fucking Prada for 9 years Ray had to have some type of feelings for her right? Ray had got on top of Prada he was beating her pussy up like he was mad. Ray could feel that he was about to cum. This pussy so good Ray told Prada. Damn this pussy is so good. Ray didn't even pull out he had no reason too. He knew for a fact he had a condom on.

Chapter 52: Agent Price, Tiffany & Lil J

Tiffany and Lil J had about 3 hours left before they made it to New York. They weren't speeding or anything. I have to pee Tiffany told Lil J. Lil J didn't want to stop however, Tiffany kept on saying she had to pee. Ok DAMN!!!!!! Lil J said were going to stop I see a "Replace Gas Station "up ahead. I'm going to stop there hurry up and go use the restroom. I'll get some gas do you want something out of the store? No Tiffany replied. About 5 minutes later Tiffany and Lil J pulled up to "The Replace Gas Station ". Tiffany jumps out and run in the store. Lil J was chilling in the car for a minute. When he looked up the car was surrounded by black vans, undercover cars, and The FBI Swat Team. Oh Shit!!!! Oh Shit!!!!!! Lil J yelled what the fuck?

GET OUT WITH YOUR HANDS UP!!!!!!!!!!!!!

GET OUT NOW!!!!!!!!!!!!!!!!!

AGENTS GO IN THE RESTROOM AND GET TIFFANY OUT OF THERE NOW!!!!!!!!!!!!!!!

Lil J was shocked and scared. He had never been in a situation like this. Knowing he had the 1 kilo he was supposed to get up North. He was fucked him and Tiffany. Damn he thought as he seen Tiffany coming out the gas station handcuff. Tiffany was yelling what's going on Lil J like she knew nothing. Lil J was yelling shut the fuck up BITCH nothing is going on. The Agents ask Lil J was there any drugs in the car? Lil J said no I don't give you permission to search the car. With that the Agents told Lil J we don't need your permission. They sat Lil J and Tiffany in the back of an undercover car. The Agent said I want you to listen to something. I'm going to close the door and go search the car.

Lil J and Tiffany listened as a voice they knew all so well came through the speakers of the car. Laughing what you mother fuckers thought you would play me? You both thought I didn't know that you two were fucking. And Tiffany I thought better of you. That's what I get for thinking right? Lil J you dumb ass nigga I knew you took money from me. Drugs from me and I knew that you had your eyes on Candy. I saw how you looked at her when she came out of my room. Well I wish you two the best. With that Chris said "Revenge Is a Mother Fucker just like you two"

Right when the tape was ending. Another tape came on this time it was Lil J and Tiffany talking in the car. All Tiffany could do was cry Lil J just put his head down and realize he sold out for a piece of pussy. Just than a tap was on the window. Well we found a total of 3 kilos in the car, 5 machine guns, 1 shot gun and about 6 ounces of weed. I think you two might as well get ready to spend the rest of your lives in a Federal Prison. Oh by the way where did you get the cocaine from? "It has a stamp on it that said Revenge Is a Mother Fucker ". Just than Lil J looked at Tiffany and said Chris set us up. How could he have out smarted us like this?

DAMN!!!!!! All of this for a piece of pussy?

Chapter 53: Chris

Chris waited and waited after the call came in about 3am.

Ring, Ring, Ring

Chris: Hello

This is Federal Agent Price we have them in Custody. Thank you for the information. I owe you one off the record. If you ever need anything hit me up.

Chris: Hung up without saying anything.

Chris set up in bed thinking about Lil J how could he cross me like this? Chris was always the type to do unto others as they have done unto him. Now they are out of the way it was time for Chris to focus on getting Candy away from Ray. Truth be told Chris really wanted to kill Lil J. However, he knew Lil J was a real pussy nigga and couldn't do any real time. A life sentence that was. Tiffany on the other hand she was weak as well. Chris was using her for his own personal reasons. Chris knew that Tiffany would cross him. He just didn't know when and how. Chris said a little Prayer and thank GOD that Tiffany wasn't as smart. She didn't even think that Chris knew her type. Chris slowly shook his head and did something he never does. Let a tear fall from his right eye. Once again the memories of his childhood attacked his brain. Chris said out aloud its life and life always goes on. Chris would find out life can be stopped at any time any moment. The one thing that Chris wasn't afraid of was dying. Chris knew the reality was he was going to one day leave this earth. Out of sight out of mind from this early morning forward. He would not think of Tiffany or Lil J. They were both dead to him. At least that is what Chris thought.

Chapter 54: Lil J & Tiffany

STATE OF NEW YORK CITY

V.S

TiFFANY A. {Tiffany} AND JOHN L. {Lil J}

Their Court Appearance December 10, 2012 at 8:00am.

Your Magistrate we have called before you Tiffany A and John L. They were caught with a total of 3 kilos in the car, 5 machine guns, 1 shot gun and about 6 ounces of weed. The Federal Bureau of Investigation was tipped off to Tiffany and John. Which they would be traveling from Down South to New York City with kilos, and guns. At that time we posted at each State Line which we have photos of Tiffany and John, GPS Tracking their every move, and wire taps that were throughout their car they were traveling in { A red Magnum }. I will present all evidence as Exhibit A. The Magistrate looked through all evidence that was submitted.

Tiffany A. I will start with you. Do you have anything to say about the evidence that was submitted against you?

Tiffany A. spoke with tears in her eyes and a running nose. Your Magistrate I'm sorry I'm so sorry. I didn't know anything I was just riding with Lil J to New York.

Lil J spoke up you lying BITCH you. You knew everything that was going on. We were fucking you BITCH.

The Magistrate listen to them fuss with one another. For about 5 minutes. They went back and forward neither one of them wanting to be in handcuffs.

The Magistrate spoke to their Public Defenders which were really working with the Magistrate, friends with the Agents in charge of the case. This is how things always were. They were all friends in Business Suits. The Magistrate sentenced them both to 30 years a piece.

The Magistrate let them know that she has placed a Rule 35 on their case. A Rule 35 means that someone anyone could come forward and put in work on their case. Meaning that if someone came forward with information that could result to someone else getting charged with a Federal Crime. Their sentence could be reduce. Dealing with the Feds it was always a win situation for the Feds not the parties involved. Everyone knew once the Federal Bureau of Investigation started a case against you. You were bound to get hung with more time than you can handle. It was crazy everyone that sold kilos got more time than a white collar crime such as robbing a bank. When the Magistrate Sentence Tiffany and John. They both went to screaming, cursing and crying. How the fuck can we do that much time you bitch. John L. yelled out. Get him out of my Courtroom before I give him an extra 10 years for talking to me like. With that said the bailiffs escorted them both out of the Courtroom.

Lil J thought to himself I'm 34 years old. This time is going to kill me I'm going to go crazy. He had only 1 person that he could call on. He had done her so wrong would she be there for him? Would she walk away? I mean 30 years that's a very long time. Would she risk her life, freedom and put in work for Lil J?

Tiffany cried for 3 weeks 30 years. What am I going to do with 30 years? Tiffany didn't have anyone to call. The one person she could call on she crossed him. Tiffany got prepared to do her time. Would she go plum crazy? Would she stand up and face 30 years? What would Tiffany do? How would she do it? Did Tiffany have information on someone that could set her free? Who was Tiffany? As we all know she was Chris girlfriend and fucking Lil J. Right?

Chapter 55: Ray and Candy

Candy went inside the house after getting dropped off. Candy wasn't as stupid and dumb as Ray thought. Candy knew exactly where Ray was going. And that was to The Pork and Pork Projects to see Prada. If Ray wanted to keep stepping out on Candy after everything they have been through. Then so be it Candy had her own plans in motion. Besides thinking about Chris and been in contact with Federal Agent Price. Candy already had one up on Ray. At least that what she was thinking. Candy wanted to speak with Chris. She grab her purse and jumped in her Grand Pix when she wanted to lay low she jumped in her Grand Pix. She jumped in her car and left. Driving about 10 minutes away from her and Ray house. She seen a pay phone on the corner. She picked the phone and dialed Chris #

Ring, Ring, Ring

Chris: Hello who this?

Candy: Hi how are you? Your voice is like music to my ears. I miss you Chris.

Chris: I miss you to Candy. I want you to know I have done my part. Tiffany is gone Lil J is gone. I need you in my life. I want a family with you Candy. Just tell me what need to be done and I will do it. I have to have you. I have been thinking about you every minute of every day. I go to sleep thinking about you.

I dream about you Candy. I need you point blink period.

Candy: Stood there with tears in her eyes. She could not believe what she was hearing. She has never heard anyone pour their heart out to her. All she ever hears from Ray are threats. That she was sure he would carry out if he had to. Candy couldn't even say anything to Chris.

Chris: Are you there? Candy I love you point blink period. Ray he has to go I have done my part and now it is time for you to do your part. My word is my bond. Without my word Candy I am nothing.

Candy: Chris I have been thinking about you as well. I really care about you. I'm torn between the two of you. Ray has done a lot of dirt to me. I have something lined up for him. I'll contact you when I get things in order. Until than know that I am thinking about you. Loving you and your in my heart and mind. With that said Candy hung before Chris could say anything else. Candy laughed I should get an Oscar for this role I'm playing. Weak ass nigga but damn that dick is so good. Candy said out loud.

Chapter 56: Agent Price and Candy

Candy hung up the phone with Chris. And dialed Agent Price

Ring, Ring, Ring,

Agent Price: Yo

Candy: Hi Agent Price this is Candy Cane. I'm ready I'll do what I need to do for Ray and I.

Agent Price: Yes!!!!!!!!! I knew you would jump on board with me. I have been Praying for you.

Candy: I'm find Agent Price thank you. Have you heard from Dr. Wan?

Agent Price: Yes I have he just called me the other day and asked me about you. I told him I would meet him in person to update him about you Candy.

Candy: I know Agent Price I know that. Well I want you to know I have information that could go ahead and seal the case. Ray has beat me again and again since you saw me in the hospital. Ray has a child on the way with this hood rat bitch name Prada. From The Pork and Pork Projects. From messing with my friend Sapphire, and Tasha. I have had enough of Ray's bullshit. I want him out of my life for a while. I don't care or love Ray anymore. I'm playing a role that I'm getting tired of playing with Ray. Agent. Price do you know Chris?

Agent Price: Yes I just did a big bust with the help of Chris.

Candy: Agent Price he is going to be my future husband. I care and love him Agent Price that is my main reason for wanting Ray out the way. With that said Candy asked Agent Price to meet her in 2 days. At the "Block on Block Coffee Shop "at 2pm. She told Agent Price that she would be wearing some red 5 inch boots, a red skirt, and a red shirt and some red shades with a red hat. She would be in her Benz Truck which was red as well.

Agent Price: Told her he would see her in 2 days. Take care

Candy: Hung up the phone.

Chapter 57: Candy.

As Candy left the pay phone. She rode in silence her mind racing a million miles per hour. Thinking about how life would be with Chris. She hopes that things would be better. Even though Ray offered Candy the good life she wanted more. All of the nice things they were nice. Candy was not a materialistic chick at all. She really hated getting dressed up all the time. Candy wanted to just be herself through it all. No matter what happened at the end of everyday Candy crave for freedom. Not just freedom from a jail cell but freedom from within. Candy wanted to be loved and love freely. Have sex with no remorse. Kiss with no regrets. That was something that she felt with Chris the one time they had sex. She felt freedom loving caring freedom. She once felt that with Ray but not anymore. Candy had grew hate towards Ray. Driving with her thoughts all over the place. She arrived back at the Mansion. Candy already knew that Ray wasn't coming home tonight again. She thought about riding to The Pork and Pork Project to confront Prada and Ray. Candy quickly rethought her thoughts took a long hot shower and laid down. Falling asleep thinking about Chris and their future together.

Chapter 58: Ray and Prada

I'm going to lay low here Prada for about 3 days. I just want to clear my mind. Prada lean over and gave Ray a kiss. That is fine with me. Ray told Prada in the morning he was going to give her some money to go and get her hair done, toes, nails, and go shopping. If Ray was going to be around Prada for the next 3 days he at least wanted her to look decent. Prada really wasn't ugly she just allowed the cocaine habit to bring her down. Ray knew all about Prada and the many dudes she had been with. Could Ray change her? The next morning Prada brought Ray some breakfast in bed. Prada was a chef she never told anyone that. Prada always thought that people would laugh at her if she told them about her many Certificates she had. Prada had a Certificate in Computer Business, She Graduated High School with Honors, and Graduated from Nail Class. That was all before she met Sonny. The dude that introduce her to Cocaine. Once Prada snorted that first line she was hooked. Then she started shooting coke. Ray told Prada the money is on the nightstand. Get you $5,000 and go and get whatever you like. Please get your hair done, nails and toes please Prada gosh. Ray set Prada down and told her it was never too late to change her ways. Prada we have been doing this for 9 years. I want you to get yourself together completely. If you show me you can get yourself together. I will get you a place, a car and take care of you. I will be there for you no matter what Ray told Prada. With that said tears started falling out of Prada's eyes. She was so sad and happy at the same time. Thank you Ray for everything for just looking after me. Everyone else they just to fuck me. Ray said listen I don't ever want you to talk about everyone else. Don't tell me what anyone has said about you. I don't want to hear anything about anything. With that said Ray gave her the keys to his hoot ride you know a car that doesn't have rims, music or anything just a typical small little car. That's a hoot ride. Prada jumped in the car with $5,000 and pressed the gas. For the next 6 hours Prada was gone shopping and enjoying herself not even thinking about cocaine. Prada was going to get herself together. She knew that her 9 years with Ray would pay off.

If anything she knew that she had a baby in her tummy and that she would be in Ray life forever. A baby would tie them together forever. Prada got her nails done, toes done and hair just as Ray requested. Prada was looking good she had got her some MAC Makeup, some clothes, a new purse, and still had money left over. She was thinking I want to get high and I mean really high. Instead Prada took the money back to Ray. Which was $2,500 Ray was still in bed chilling and watching T.V. Hi Ray I missed you when I was gone. Thank you again Ray for everything. Prada was looking good to Ray and he wanted to fuck her. Come here Prada I like the way you look. With that said Ray grab her face and kissed her dead in the mouth. That shocked Prada and him. Ray was falling for Prada and had been falling hard for her. Ray fucked Prada without a condom for the first time. And for some reason Ray told her you need to go to the Doctor. Are you Pregnant? Prada told him no not that I know of. Knowing good and well she knew that was pregnant. What will she find out once she went to the Doctor? A Doctor that Ray had requested that she go and see? Ray sent her to the Dr. Chin Lang, in less than 2 hours. She was back with her paperwork she was pregnant which she knew already. She was 4 weeks pregnant. Prada took Ray the paperwork and he was not happy at all. He told her you have to have an abortion. I'll pay for it Prada started to cry no Ray I don't want to have an abortion I really want this child our child. Ray looked at her and felt a weak spot for her. Prada I will think about it. Come here give me a hug. With that said they laid down and went to sleep. Ray was thinking I'm going to be a father. He thought about Candy for a minute she can't give me a family. Ray thought a father for the 1st time. I'm going to be the best dad in the world Ray thought to himself. If this BITCH Prada try to use my baby against me I will kill her myself and I mean that. Ray was thinking eventually he fail off to sleep wrapped up with Prada. Would Ray be around to see the birth of his 1st child?

Chapter 59: Agent Price & Candy

Candy arrived at "The Block and Block "coffee shop at 1:59pm. Agent price was already seated in the right corner of the shop. Candy walked in like she owned the place. Giving Agent Price a huge hug. Hi it is nice to see you again said Agent Price. The feelings are mutual. Let's get straight to business. That was something about Candy she was not the one to bullshit. Candy didn't even order anything from the Coffee shop. She pulled out a Vanilla Envelope. She told Agent Price this is everything you need right here. To close your case. I have Ray's location in the paperwork. I do not want my name listed on anything. I have the title to my Trucks their both in my name. I want to keep those their mind. I know you all have to take the mansion and that is fine with me. I don't care I'm going to need something else from you but I'll get back in touch with you soon. With that said Candy got up Agent Price stood up and hugged her again. She walked away jumping in her Benz Truck. Before she started the truck up notice someone looking at her really hard. Candy was so deep in she knew that couldn't be touched by anyone. There was no way everyone in all the high places loved her. With those thoughts she started her Benz Truck and pulled off.

Chapter 60: Agent Price

Agent Price just set there thinking to himself. How amazing Candy was she had really grown. No one knew the truth about how Agent Price really knew Candy. Agent Price had been looking for Candy for a very long time. Once he seen her in the Hospital she knew who she was. Agent Price was Candy's brother. Agent Price was Lauren Candy's mother older son. Agent. Price was Lauren's their mother first child. Agent Price never lived with Lauren. His father some dude that Candy never met raised him. Agent Price knew he had a little sister he just didn't want to bring heat on her by contacting his sister Candy. The blue car that was watching and following Candy was Agent Price. He would never tell Candy who he really was. He would just keep that a secret until the day he died. With those thoughts Agent Price got up and left "The Block and Block "coffee shop. He arrived back at The Federal Building where he went through the Vanilla Envelopes. Enclosed were the following items to put the icing on the cake and bring Ray down.

1} Video tapes of Ray cooking dope.

2} All of the information on his over sees Accounts, Real Estate Property,

3} Names and addresses of everyone that Ray was connected to including the Mexican Cartel.

4} Ray loading guns in the trunk of his car.

5} Ray wrapping up kilos and kilos of cocaine

6} to really seal the deal Candy had wire tapped the inside of Ray's car.

7} Ray's location right at this minute

Agent Price just laughed and said out loud. That is my little sister. She isn't even playing with Rayshawn B. Jones. Everything that Candy had given Agent Price. Plus the evidence he already had. Agent Price was ready to make an arrest.

Chapter 61: Candy

Candy drove back to the mansion. Went to the safe and got out all the money which was in the safe. It was a total not including drugs of 5 million dollars in the safe. Candy filled her bag up walked around the house for the last time. Made sure she had the titles to her trucks and left the house. Vowing to never step foot in the house again. Candy jumped in her truck and went to Miami where she got her a penthouse suite in the Trump Towers. Starting rate for a penthouse suite was $4,000 a night. Candy booked her suite for 2 weeks for a total of $56,000. Once she got on the 200th floor and went into her Penthouse Suite. Candy jumped up and down on the bed yelling running naked through the Penthouse Suite. I'm free I'm free thank you God I'm free. I don't have to deal with Ray's bullshit anymore. And to think he thought I didn't know about Prada's plan.

What's going to happen next...?

Chapter 62: Candy & Chris

Candy settled down and called Chris.

Ring, Ring. Ring,

Chris: Hello

Candy: Hi how are you? I miss you. I need you I want you in my life. Come to me I have a Penthouse Suite in Miami. Come on let's go everything is taken care of on my end.

Chris: I'm on my way I love you Candy.

Candy: I love you as well.

They both hung up.

Chris she did it finally I have been waiting on that call. Chris already had his duffle bag full of money packed and ready. All he was waiting on was the call from Candy. He thought she would never call. He grab his duffle bag which contained 20 million dollars jumped in his car and hit the express way. Heading to Miami the Trump Towers.

9 hours later Chris arrived. Happy excited and feeling loved even before he got up to the 200th floor. He got on the elevator and took it up to the 200th floor. With his duffle bag full of money.

Knock, Knock, Knock

Candy let him in jumping into his arms. I love you Chris was spinning her around. I love you too. I missed you so much it seems like it has been forever since I last saw you Candy. I thought that you would never call me. Why would you think that asked Candy? Without my word I'm nothing like you told me. With that said they made sweet love and relaxed talked about their dreams, goals, and if they wanted kids and everything else in between. Candy felt really good for the first in a long time. That night would be one of the best nights of her life. She had Chris, her

new found freedom and millions to go along with everything
else.

Chapter 63: Agent Price, Ray, & Prada

Agent Price and his crew were preparing to go to The Pork and Pork Projects. Ray was so caught up in Prada he didn't even notice that Candy had left from The City and took all his money that was in the safe. Ray hadn't even picked up the phone to call Candy. And that was fine with Candy she knew it was just a matter of time before Agent Price gave her the call that she has been waiting for. Candy was tired of role playing with Ray. Every night everyday role playing gaming trying to remember every little detail, never forgetting to take notes, press play on the necklace she always wore that had a camera installed in it. Candy was just tired of it. She must admit though at one point and time she actually loved and cared about Ray.

Agent Price are we ready boys? It's apartment #404. It's 5:30am they should be snoring at this time. Little did they know Prada was up throwing up morning sickness from the baby.

Boom!! Boom!!! Boom!!!

Federal Agents FBI get down on the ground now. Don't look at us they bust the door down. Had they guns drawn and was ready for war with whoever didn't listen to their demands.

Ray was shocked how did they know he was there? Is this the day that Ray had tried to avoid? Prada don't say anything I'll get us a Lawyer.

Agent Price stated oh don't worry Ray and Prada you will need one. We have so much evidence on you Ray. Prada you just had to fuck with old Ray'Shawn B. Jones didn't you? Asked Agent Price. Prada couldn't say anything. Don't looked shocked baby girl everything is going to be fine once you start talking. Ray yelled out don't say anything Prada. I'm going to call Candy and explain everything to her. I'll have her get the money out the safe and come bond me out of jail. Once I get out I'll come back and get you Prada. Trust me on this one Prada please.

Prada had her own set of rules and that was to not trust anyone including herself.

Prada just stood there in handcuffs crying. What has she got herself in?

Agent Price let Ray know. Ray Candy is gone I would have thought that you knew that. I see you wouldn't know anything about anything been that you have been here for the last 2 ½ days. Have you even called Candy? Nope you didn't call her your phone has been tapped by us for a long time.

Take them Downtown to the Federal Building and book them.

I have a surprise for the both of you. Agent Price informed Ray and Prada. Something that is going to shock you. I might just have to call the Ambulance to be on the scene just in case 1 of you have a heart attack.

Agent Price stayed behind to see what else he could find in Prada Apartment. Agent Price didn't find much of anything. A paper from a Doctor stating that she was pregnant 4 weeks.

Damn!!!! Agent Price said to himself. This is going to be crazy really crazy.

Chapter 64: Chris & Candy

Later on that night after going to sleep and waking back up. They realized it was 7am they had more sex ordered room service and ate breakfast. Chris fed Candy some strawberries and chocolate. Later on that day around 3pm they received a call from Agent Price.

Ring, Ring, Ring

Chris get that for me please Candy yelled from the shower.

Hello: Hi Chris long time no hear from.

Chris: Didn't catch the voice right off. Who's speaking?

Agent Price how are you?

Chris: What's up man? What's going on? Do you have that news for us?

Agent Price: Of course I do you know I handle my business. I just wanted to call and let you two know that you can do what you need to do from here.

Chris: I'm going to let Candy know we already know the deal.

Agent Price hung up the phone.

Chris walked in and got in the shower with Candy. Butt naked looking thick and dick hanging not to long but many steps up from Ray's little ass dick. Candy just smiled what's up baby? Candy asked Chris you already know. That was Agent Price he said it's done. Everything is lined up and ready to go. With that said Chris bent down and ate Candy's pussy why she stood up. Leaning against the wall in the shower and the water beating down on their bodies she came in Chris mouth and he kept licking and sucking slowly on her spur tongue. His dick was hard as a rock. He stuck it in Candy's pussy from the back and they made love in the shower. About 10 minutes of slowly making love and crying tears of joy and happiness. They both came together. Not even knowing that at that moment Chris sperm met 1 of Candy's eggs. That would equal a baby that was conceive in the Trump Towers Penthouse Suite in the shower. They both got out of the shower dried off and prepared for a day of fun in Miami Beach. They went shopping, to the beach, swimming with the Dolphins, They went to the spa, out to eat at a 5 star restaurant, after about 7 hours of fun they were both tired. They went back to the Penthouse Suite and fall fast asleep.

Chapter 65: Agent Price, Ray and Prada

Back in the Federal Building in the City. Agent Price was trying to get information of out Ray. Ray wasn't talking or answering no questions. In the other room Prada had went against everything that Ray had told her. Prada was talking she was trying to talk her out of doing any time. The things that Prada was saying was not helping her at all. Only hurting her and making things worst for the both of them. Prada was crying, shaking and throwing up.

Agent Price told her that there is no need for all of that. I have something for you and Ray. Something that is going to be really good. I can't wait until the time comes. I just want to show you a thing or two. Let you both know how I get down. I'm not about to play with you Prada. You have gotten herself in over your head. How was the shopping trip that you took the other week? With Ray's money? What was it $5,000 that he gave you? Prada looked up with tears on her eyes. How did you know that? Prada I know everything about everything. I know that your Grandma, Granddad took care of you. Your mother treated you like shit growing up. You were dirty and reeked of piss. I know all about you Prada. How you were fucking since you was 10 years old. What a shame you have had a rough life. I guess you thought that Ray would come and save the day. You should have just kept snorting your personal cocaine. No you thought you moved up a notch when you started sucking Ray's little old dick. I know all about him I have heard many of young girls talking bad about his dick. If Ray didn't have money, drugs and cars what would Ray be? Who would Ray be? Think about that Prada. Would you have even fucked with Ray? I know that you put holes in the condom to get pregnant with Ray's child. Does Ray know that? I think not I know he doesn't know that. Ray would have killed you Prada. Just think about it you have been fucking, sucking and snorting Ray's cocaine for how long? 9 long years and he is just now trying to make you his wife. His main girlfriend how fucking dumb can you be Prada? I'm going to put you up on game only because I feel sorry for you. Ray knew that we were on to him, Ray came to your house for 3 days because he knew that we would soon bust him. Ray didn't call Candy and wanted you to believe that he would leave Candy alone for you. Prada listen Ray loves Candy with everything in him. No matter what Ray told you or the fact that he kissed you in the mouth for the first time. Ray is a Kingpin a major Kingpin. Ray is a role player and baby girl I'm sorry to inform you but Ray has played you, fucked you and is going to leave you with a child to have in a Federal Prison. I'm going to leave you Prada in this room for a while and let you think about things.

On another note***********

Chapter 66: Ray

Ray was in the next room sweating bullets by now. He already knew that Agent Price was going to go and tear Prada apart. Agent Price fed Prada lies everything that Agent Price told Prada it was a lie. Prada didn't know that the Agents, Police, and under covers could do that. They could lie to get their information. Prada should have listened to Ray and kept her mouth shut. Damn!!!!! I know this bitch is going to talk I just know it. Damn!!!!!! Ray went to thinking where is Candy? He haven't heard from her in a long time. Just than a light came on in Ray's mind.

CANDY SET ME UP THAT FUCKING BITCH SET ME UP. Ray went to yelling   NO!!!!!!!!!!   NO!!!!!!!!!!!!!!!!!!!! NO!!!!!!!!!!!!!!!!!

How could she do me like this? There was no way that Agent Price could have known that's where I was located unless he was watching me. Let me calm down Candy did told me they were watching me. Maybe I should have believed her instead of thinking she was high off cocaine. Damn!!!!!!! My mind is playing tricks on me. Candy she is my wife she is loyal to me. I have her marching to my beat like she is in a band. I control her that is my property Ray thought to himself. She wouldn't cross me. It was something that stuck in the back of Ray's mind though. Agent Price it seemed like he had his own hidden agenda he wants my head on a platter Ray thought to himself. It was something that Ray couldn't figure out what it was. It was heavy on his mind. Damn!!!! I can't put my finger on it. I know Agent Price from somewhere but where? Ray set in the cold room handcuffed to the table for what seemed like 24 hours. It was only 10 hours.

Chapter 67: Chris and Candy

The next morning Chris and Candy got up.

Good Morning Thank you Lord for waking us up. I love you Chris Candy said.

Chris said the same thing.

They got up took a shower, made love put their clothes on. And check out of the Trump Towers 4 days early. Everything was falling right in place. They went to a car lot and sold Chris car for $500.00 dollars. And prepared to take the 9 hour trip back to the City. Once in the City they knew to go straight to the Federal Building and meet with Agent Price. They knew they had to park where the workers of the Federal Building parked at. Call Agent Price once they arrived. They were on the express way riding out. Holding hands and listening to their favorite song Must Be Nice By: Life Jennings. 8 hours later they arrived at the Federal Building. Candy was driving fast she was excited. About what?

Candy dialed up Agent Price.

Ring, Ring, Ring,

Agent Price: Hello

Candy: We have arrived. I know I'm an hour early. I'm so excited Candy told Agent. Price

Agent Price: I'll meet you at the steel yellow door in 5 minutes. Grab your bags and come to the door.

They both hung up without saying much more.

Chris what did he say babe? He said they would meet us at the yellow steel door. Are you ready Chris? Candy asked him. Yes babe I'm ready to show them what were made of.

This is where things are about to get really twisted!!!

Chapter 68: Chris, Candy, Prada, Ray, and Agent Price

As Chris and Candy met Agent Price at the door. He let them in prior to that Agent Price had moved Prada and Ray out to the lobby area. Where they could sit and see everyone that comes in and out. Chris was carrying his 20 million and Candy was carrying her 2 million.

Walking up together holding hands Chris and Candy turned left and there they were. Ray and Prada. Prada looked up through her swollen eyes. OMG!!!!!!!!!! NO!!!!!!!!!!!!!!!

Not Chris and Candy. Ray went to yelling what the fuck is going on here? What the fuck are you doing with this nigga Candy? What the fuck is happening.

Agent Price said calm the fuck down you dumb mother fuckers. Chris was standing there smiling really laughing in the inside at Ray. This nigga is about to do a lifetime little do he know. And I have his wife and his money.

Little did Chris know*********

Agent Price walked up and told Chris to drop his bag. Chris looked at him and said what? Dude stop playing your my boy. Agent Price Said Chris P. Williams. You need to follow my direct orders and drop your motherfucking bag. Put your hands behind your back. You're under arrest. Chris yelled for fucking what? What the fuck did I do?

Little did Prada know********

Prada was still crying. Prada Agent Price told her. Honey you're not pregnant at all. The Dr. Lang you went and seen she is really a Federal Agent she works for us. With that said the fake Doctor came from around the corner. Hi again Prada I'm sorry to inform you that was fake paperwork that I gave you. Prada looked shocked what the fuck is going on here? Prada said out loud.

Little did Ray know*********

Agent Price walked up to Ray and took the cuffs off of him. They shook hands you did really well Ray. You're a season vet to this game. The Federal Agents told me that you and Candy would get these players off the streets. You did a real good job with that said Ray walked up to Candy and kissed her in the mouth. He turned back and looked at Chris and said her pussy good and tight isn't it. You liked her pussy and head didn't you Chris. Listen this was business it wasn't nothing personal. You just got caught slipping. What did you think that Candy would turn on me for you? Nigga please no matter how big your dick is and how good you fuck her. Her love and loyalty is with me forever. And my love and loyalty is with her. Chris was boiling hot he had given up his friend and everything for Candy. He had turned in Tiffany the one person he knew was down for him for a fact. With those thoughts someone that Chris had wrote off long time ago. Came from behind the corner.

IT WAS TIFFANY!!!!!!! YES Tiffany that was sentence to 30 years with Lil J. Tiffany and Candy were sister's yes that's right they were sisters. Tiffany was Candy little sister that she had never met before. How did they know they were sisters than? That would make Ray Tiffany brother in law. When Agent. Price blocked Candy off and told her. He had enough evidence against her and Ray and they were both facing a life sentence. That is when Candy put her money to use to find out who her little sister really was. That's when she found out that Tiffany was her little lost sister. And she was fucking Chris and Lil J the two people that Agent Price really wanted. When Agent Price told Candy she had to become an Informant. She contacted Tiffany and told her what was going on with her and Ray. Tiffany jumped right on board with her big sister Candy. There was no way Tiffany was going to allow the Feds to take her only sister away from her. The big sister Tiffany had always wanted in her life. WOW!!!! Tiffany told Candy once Candy told her that her and Ray were facing a life sentence. You got damn right I will help you big sis Tiffany said. Ray didn't even much know that Candy and Tiffany were sisters. After they met for the first time Candy and Tiffany they became tighter than super glue. No one in the world could come between the love they had for one another. And when I mean no one I mean no one. No nigga, No hoe, No Agent or anything. Candy and Tiffany they were two different people with one mission. To keep Candy and Ray out of the Federal Penitentiary. So there stood Ray, Candy and Tiffany.

Prada was still thinking how did I come into play? She looked up with the swollen eyes and asked Ray. Ray so you never loved me or anything. Ray told her no not at all I actually hated you. Baby girl it's nothing personal you aren't my type at all. Look at you really think that $5,000 I gave you was something didn't you. Prada baby I'm worth more than $100 Million Dollars. Candy and Tiffany both laughed at Chris and Prada. You all really thought your game was good didn't you? Agent Price told Chris. Chris was boiling hot bitch I'm going to find you and kill you Chris shouted. I'm going to get out one day and find you and destroy you. Candy, Tiffany and Ray all laughed. I see you don't know any better do you. How long have you been serving dope Chris? All of your life and your 34 what the fuck have you learned? Nothing right if you learned anything you wouldn't be sitting here about to do this life sentence. Were about to ball on your 20 million. Candy, Ray and Tiffany stated you will never be able to find us. Our names are Candy, Ray, Tiffany with that said they grab 2 duffle bags. And turned to walk away.

Chris yelled at Candy to stop. Candy told Ray and Tiffany and Agent Price to wait on her. She went back to see what he wanted. Chris looked at her with tears in her eyes. Did you love me Candy? Candy looked at him and one tear failed for her eye. Chris I didn't love you at all. I'm a role player this is something I had to do. Chris understand something I would have loved you. I would have been loyal to you just as I am loyal to Ray and Tiffany. Even though I just found out Tiffany is my little lost sister. I knew that Agent Price wanted you and Lil J. You two were on his target list. However, I was already in too deep. My loyalty and love is with Ray. I could never cross him if I wanted to. I just couldn't cross Ray. All of the evidence you thought I gave them on Ray. Chris that was evidence against you. I helped them put you here. I had no other choice Chris. The watch I gave you Chris it had a camera in it. Everything they have against you is true. Don't go to trial Chris whatever you do don't go to trial with the FBI. This is my life it was either yours or ours. I couldn't leave my sister out here in a cold world like this. Chris you thought you would just do my little sister any kind of way. You tried to play my little sister once I found out she was my little sister it was only right that we turned the table on you. With that said Candy wiped her tears and said Chris I'm sorry I'm really sorry. When you crossed Lil J you took
20

years off Ray Sentence. When I crossed you I took 20 years off my Sentence. When Ray put Prada in the cross fire it took a total of 5 years a piece off our Sentence. So that means together we had 50 years total took off our Sentence. 25 years a piece Chris this is the life that we have choose to live. You didn't think it would end up like this. You never thought for once I would cross you. Candy walked away leaving Chris in his own thoughts. And to do his own time. Tiffany is really Candy's sister I would have never thought that in a million years Chris said out loud. Chris set back handcuffed to the chair. Thinking how in the fuck did this happen?

Chapter 69: Agent Price, Candy, Ray & Tiffany

They were all walking through the back door of the Federal Building. When they stopped in Agent Price Office. It has been a pleasure working you 3 Agent Price told them. We have been trying to get Chris and Lil J off the streets for about three years now. You all came and got them off the streets in less than a year. You three are a force to be reckon with. With that said Candy pulled Agent Price to the side. I just wanted to thank you for everything. There is really no way I can ever re pay you for everything you have done for me, Tiffany and Ray. Agent Price I have something to give you. I asked that you not reject my gift. With that said Candy pulled out 2 million dollars and the titles to her two Trucks that Ray had brought her. Candy said Agent Price before you say anything I want you to know that I know that your my older brother. I know that our Mother Lauren had you and you went to stay with your Father leaving me behind. This is our younger sister Tiffany, with that said Tiffany stepped up it's nice to finally meet you Agent Brother Price. Agent Price couldn't say anything. Tiffany said I want you to take this to our Mother. Let her know that were doing well you seen us. Give her the titles to my two trucks and the title to the Mansion. Ray and I have already signed over everything in her name. All she has to do is sign her name on the Documents. Let her know that we will be in touch with her when time permits. Contact our Aunt Minnie here is her # {333}666-1111. Give her this 1 million for my baby girl. Let her know I said thank you for everything. This should help her out tell her I said tell my baby girl. I love and I will never ever forget about her never. I need you to give my best friend Diamond $300,000. Tell her I said thanks for everything. Let her know I'm doing well. I met my little sister Tiffany finally. I'm still going hard with Ray's crazy ass. Tell her I can't get in contact with her for her protection but I will always carry her in my heart. With that said they all hugged and cried. Agent Price you're a wonderful person and brother. I wish you nothing but the best. Candy and Tiffany told their brother. Agent Price gave Ray, Candy and Tiffany a Vanilla Envelope. They already knew what the contents were. Agent Price walked them outside where a Private Jet was waiting on them to board. It was nice to meet you take care and tell mama we love her Tiffany and Candy said. Agent Price shook Ray's hand and said you are a real gamer. I see you taught my sister Candy well. Take care of my sisters if you need anything. They both said together call me.

Chapter 70: Tiffany, Candy & Ray

Once they were on the Private Jet. They jumped up and hugged 1 another. They were 26 million dollars richer. They set down and put their seat belts on. They all open up their envelopes. Enclosed was a letter from Agent Price.

I just wanted to thank you three for the work you put in to help us get Lil J and Chris. You guys are some real role players. The next destination you three will be going to is Missouri. Once you arrive there you need to locate

The Federal Building

333 Federal Road

Missouri, Missouri 1111

{777}888-9999 Agent Ransom will be your contact Agent. Call him if you get lost.

I have enclosed your new identities. Including Social Security Cards, Birth Certificates, Id's, and Driving License. For all 3 of you. With the 50 years that was knocked off for working to get Chris and Lil J off the streets. You only need 10 more years that would be 20 years together and you guys will be free. To do as you please. Candy, Tiffany & Ray you all have my best wishes. Stay safe and if you need anything feel free to call me. I almost forgot to mention that Lil J he hung himself he couldn't handle the 30 years The Magistrate gave him. They found him at 3:00am hanging by a sheet.

I guess the saying is true only the strong will survive in the game of life.

You either playing or getting played. Either way you have to be careful. You will never the real identities of the players in the game. Or how the dice can land. Always remain cautious you never know when your time will come or who will cross you.

Some people you can never forget if you wanted to. Their embedded in your heart and soul. I'll never forget you Candy thought to herself about Chris. My love, loyalty, honor will always be with Ray'shawn B. Jones. We're connected in more ways than anyone will ever know.

By Any Means.....

C. Tanae

Mysterious Girl Publishing:

Coming soon:

A look into By Any Means Necessary...

Mysterious Girl Publishing:

By Any Means Necessary.

Once they arrived at the Missouri Airport.

Candy was Sheila

Ray was Mike

Tiffany Misty

If you heard their names over the phone. You would think they were upper class white people. Sheila, Mike and Misty. They already knew their roles and what needed to be done. At this point they were told who they were to go after. Some Random dude and his chick that goes by the name Preston and A'raya. They were a major power couple, there were into weed and making counterfeit Money. The Agents had been after this power couple for more than 5 years. Agent Ransom told the trio I heard you all have been making some major moves when it comes to helping us. I just wanted to take this time out to thank you.

The Agents gave them 2 years max to get it done. Sheila said were trying to get this done in less than six months. We have plans this is our last time snitching on anyone. I'm ready to make this one last move and go on with my life. Agent Ransom said I understand that Sheila. And once again we thank you three for everything. We already have you a house right next door to this power couple. We had to relocate the family that was staying in the home. We had painters paint, People laying new carpet the whole 9 yards. So Preston and A'raya wouldn't think anything was up. The Agents pulled out photos of Preston and A'raya. What? Sheila said Preston was white as rice and A'raya was black. Damn no wonder you guys can't caught them. He is white and she is black. With that said Sheila passed the pictures around the table to Mike and Misty. Everything is ready to go in the Rider Truck. Agent Ransom told the three. You have a spending limit of $30,000 at "The Company" it is a furniture store located in the upper end of Missouri. You three are going to enjoy your stay here rather it is 2 months, 6 months or 2 years. With that said Sheila and Mike turned over their duffle bags containing the 26 million dollars. That was one luxury of been an Informant. What money you make and find you get to keep. Right now between the three of them they had 26 million. The only thing once you get a Federal Case against you. And you become an Informant you have to move around so much. You can't stay in one place for a long period of time. As we all know with the right price anyone in the world can be found stinking. Agent Ransom gave them the keys to the house, and the Rider Truck. Sheila, Mike, and Misty were on their way. Leaving what had just happen with Chris and Prada behind them. Will Chris and Prada remain a memory in their life?

By Any Means Necessary..

C. Tanae

coming soon.

A letter from The Author *C. Tanae*

I would like to take this time out to thank My Lord Savior Jesus Christ. Without the strength that comes from the Lord there was no way I was going to be able to write this book. Thank you from the bottom of my heart to all my readers. I have always dreamed of becoming an Author. As we know from reading this story and by going through things in life. Life offers many twist and turns. No matter what your dreams are. You have to stay motivated and focus. If you get off track for whatever reason pray hard and get back on track and go even harder. Don't never give up on your dreams. If you want to dance, dance like you never danced before, you want to sing, sing like you're the only singer in the whole wide world. If you want to become a writer, Get your paper and pen and write until your fingers and hand become numb. Don't allow your dreams to die. When one door close always remember that 2 more doors will open. Blessings are always right around the corner. No matter who you ask for help and their not willing to help you. Stay focus google does work wonders when trying to find out information. It took me a lot of years to stop everything and write, type and Self-Publish By Any Means. I'm in the process of writing By Any Means Necessary the ending of By Any Means. The way By Any Means Necessary will end is going to shock not only you but me as well.

Follow your dreams, reach high for the stars, if you fall down and skin your knees get back up and try again. With that said the sky is the limit.

Thank you for reading

By Any Means. Written By: *C. Tanae*

I dedicate By Any Means to the three most beautiful people. I have ever met. My Angels may all your dreams come true.

Always C. Tanae